THE
Venetian's
WIFE

THE VENETIAN'S WIFE

A STRANGELY *sensual* TALE OF

A RENAISSANCE *explorer,* A *computer,*

AND A *metamorphosis*

by NICK BANTOCK

RAINCOAST BOOKS

Vancouver

First published in Canada in 1996 by
Raincoast Book Distribution Ltd.
8680 Cambie Street
Vancouver, B.C. v6p 6m9
(604) 323-7100

CANADIAN CATALOGUING IN PUBLICATION DATA

Bantock, Nick.
    The Venetian's wife

        ISBN 1-55192-027-1
        I. Title.
    PR6052.A54V46 1996   823'.914   C96-910039-6

10 9 8 7 6 5 4 3 2 1

First published in U.S.A. in 1996 by Chronicle Books.

Thanks to:
Doris Wiener of the Doris Wiener Gallery for providing the Parvati,
Roger Berg for finding Tafur,
Barbara Hodgson and Erika Berg for propping me up,
The man on the plane who told me all about Ganesha, the remover of obstacles,
And a very special thanks to Amy Poster, curator of Asian Art at the Brooklyn Museum,
        for the inside information.

The photograph of the Parvati on page 120 was provided by Mr. Richard Goodbody.
Photographs on pages 46, 56, and 119 are by Bruce Law.
Photographs of the artwork were taken by Smith Photo.
Byzantium would like to thank the team at Chronicle Books, including Annie Barrows,
        Karen Silver, Michael Carabetta, and Andrea Hirsh.

Book and cover design: Barbara Hodgson/Byzantium Books Inc.
Composition: Byzantium Books Inc.
Cover illustration: Nick Bantock

Printed in China.

TO CECILY AND GERALD GODFREY

who sowed

the first

seed

THE
*V*ENETIAN'S
WIFE

The year is 1469. Niccolo Dei Conti stands atop the steep hill that overlooks his villa on the outskirts of Venice. He clenches his fists, raises his arms to the heavens and bellows with anger and frustration at the storm raging around him. He demands that the lightning strike him down and rid him of his old age and loneliness. The storm is unobliging.

Soaked to the skin and exhausted, he returns to his lifeless villa and enters via the kitchen, leaving behind him the open door. He sits at the worn table and stares out at the night, ignoring the thunder claps, blinking only when the flashes of brilliant white light fill the door frame.

He's considering the solitude of his wifeless bed when a visitor arrives. She moves like Mercury, circling the room, touching with golden fingers the pots, pans, candle holders and all things metal. She discovers the knife that Niccolo Dei Conti's hand rests on, and because his feet are firmly planted on the floor she burns out his heart.

Niccolo Dei Conti has his wish; lightning has separated his spirit from his tired body. But his journey is not over. He has been a traveler all his life and he still has far to go.

It happened again. Stopped in the India Room to look at that Shiva drawing. The second I laid eyes on it I started to sweat. My legs went rubbery and my heart started pumping frantically. I had the disconcerting sensation that four hands were stroking and examining my body. I know it lasted only a few seconds but it felt eternal.

After the hands were gone I was very shaky. I glanced over my shoulder at the guard in the corner seat. He was looking squinty at me. I could feel my face flush, and I panicked and rushed out of the room.

I must stay away from that picture.

Getting aroused always has been pointless for me.

From: Mr. N. Conti contifnd@secset.com
To: Sara Wolfe swintrw@adl.com

Ms. Wolfe,

I couldn't help but notice how fascinated you were by the Reverend Charles Bacon's drawing of the Deccan Shiva. It has a deal of power, does it not?

Thought you might like to see this page from Bacon's personal notebook. If you find it intriguing, I'd be happy to furnish you with additional information.

N. Conti

Shiva's powers. However disquieting the implications of such a possibility, I am none the less obliged to conclude that the embodiment is no illusion.

How this passionate transfiguration was achieved is beyond my ken, and to dwell on that matter would be conjecture of the idlest sort. Better I concentrate on the Living Shiva as a spiritual message.

It is odd, and, I admit, shamefully amusing to think how scandalized my poor parishioners would be to find their good vicar not only delving into pagan mythology but championing a deity that counts amorous power among his chief attributes.

Shiva Nataraja, Lord of Dance, holds in his upper hand the drum that beats out the rhythm of creation. In his upper left, the flame of destruction. The lower right gestures benediction, and the fourth hand points to his upraised left foot, showing freedom from rebirth. His right foot crushes the demon of ignorance whilst his body is encircled by the fire of the cosmos.

to the rhythm of our blood

The living Shiva of Deccan dances through my

This is embarrassing.

Is this embarrassing?

Maybe it isn't.

Someone else must have been in the room while I was looking at the Shiva. Could he have guessed what was going on inside me? Surely not. It wasn't as if I gave any outward signs of turmoil until I was leaving. The guard was the only person I was aware of in the room. This Conti person must have come and gone while I fixated on the drawing. How does he know who I am? I guess it would have been easy enough to figure out that I work for the museum and then he could easily get my name. That's hardly alarming. I'm just feeling self-conscious because of my response to the Shiva.

Bacon page is interesting. Particularly the first two lines. What does "embodiment" imply? I presume Bacon made his drawings from the original sculpture. I wonder where that is now? Could Bacon have owned it? I'm curious. I have Mr. Conti's E-mail address; I could contact him and ask for more information.

What if he could tell what was happening to me? No, I've already decided that's not possible. Why am I such a coward? Of course I can ask him about Reverend Bacon's odd notebook.

If the museum work was half as intriguing as this Bacon thing I'd be perfectly happy, but it isn't. God! I swear I'm going to take a scalpel to the next second-rate canvas I'm asked to "conserve" all over. To have spent four grueling years studying classical painting techniques and chemistry just to be told to salvage mediocre Victorian portraits is downright demeaning. Surely I can put my eyes and brain to better use. At least I can keep my own images alive in here.

Awake by four a.m. again. I wish I slept better.
Five hours' sleep just isn't enough. These middle of
the night conversations with myself are so
inane. It doesn't matter if I pay the phone
bill by mail or in person, nor will the universe implode if I fail to paint the door
the perfect shade of blue.

What am I avoiding?

From: S. Wolfe swintrw@adl.com
To: Mr. N. Conti contifnd@secset.com

Mr. Conti,
Thank you for the unusual document. It is kind of you to have taken notice
of my interest in the Deccan Shiva. Yes, I would like to know more about
both the drawing and the Reverend Bacon. Who was he? Are there further
pages? And if you don't consider it overly prying, I'd like to ask how you
know about this piece—the museum has the drawing listed as Artist
Unknown.

Yours,
Sara Wolfe

From: Mr. N. Conti contifnd@secset.com

To: Sara Wolfe swintrw@adl.com

Ms. Wolfe,

I wish to offer you a job.

It is a peculiar response to your request for more information, I realize, but I ask you to consider my proposal with an open mind.

I know a degree about you from my formal inquiries (I hope you don't mind, but I couldn't risk error). And your response encouraged me to conclude that you're exactly the person I'm looking for.

My needs are uncomplicated. I wish to employ a bright, able-bodied person with the right kind of eye to help me locate some very specific art works.

You fit those requirements admirably, and I'm inclined to believe that you are at a stage in your career where you need an extra challenge. Also, your preoccupation with the Shiva suggested a sympathy above and beyond mere academic interest.

The job I'm offering you will require resourcefulness, imagination, willingness to travel, plus a deep love of artifact. The salary would be substantially higher than the one you receive at present.

Also, I would have you supplied with a new computer system. Travel for me is no longer possible and as the computer is my chosen method of conducting business, I would require you to have a compatible system.

I don't think I've misjudged your potential for change. And I look forward to hearing from you again.

As for the Bacon notes: Yes, there are more, but I will withhold them as an additional temptation. Being a very old man I have no problem indulging myself in a little harmless emotional blackmail when it suits my purpose.

Yours very respectfully,

N. Conti

I cannot deny it. I am ready for change. And yes I do find this offer of a new job exciting. But can I really be taking this seriously? I haven't a clue who this man is. What proof do I have that it's not a hoax? I hate the idea of being made a fool of.

Admittedly, the Bacon page seemed real enough and Mr. Conti's quirky approach to employee selection is endearingly different.

I could write again, sort of noncommittally, and ask for more information about the offer. That way I might get a better idea of how genuine this all is.

I can't believe I'm doing this.

Mother phoned to say that she and Tom were back from Maui and were thinking of buying a condo there. The only way they could afford to do that would be to sell the house. I wish Dad were here to stop her. He rebuilt that place single-handed. It's bad enough Tom living there, but the thought of the family losing the house altogether makes me feel positively sick. Even Mother couldn't trade our home in for never-ending happy hour.

I'm taking this too seriously. After all, she'll never get around to doing it. It's another of her pipe-dreams.

Going up to the plaster room this morning, I heard a noise coming from a window alcove down the hallway. I thought maybe another pigeon's got in, oh hell I'm going to have to try and usher it back out of the window, I hate all that panic and flutter.

I moved cautiously, not wanting to frighten it any further, but when I put my head around the corner, there was no bird—only Marco pouring out a bowl of chocolate milk for a big old ginger cat that was jumping down from the windowsill. From the way they greeted one another it was obvious they were old acquaintances. I remembered that I'd often seen Marco buying chocolate milk at the deli during lunch break but I'd never seen him drink it.

Marco and his friend were mewing at one another and I suddenly felt uncomfortable watching the intimacy between the ancient cat and my crouched workmate. I retraced my steps down the hallway as silently as I was able. I was sure Marco hadn't heard me, but later in the registrar's meeting I noticed him staring at me, and when our eyes met, he looked away. It's not the first time he's done that so I can't be sure if he knew I'd seen him petting his companion.

We've worked together for close to two-and-a-half years and I doubt if we've passed ten words, but I'm always aware when he's in the room. I remember how he tried to talk to me when I first arrived at the museum but I felt so shy I could barely respond, and he gave up almost immediately. Idiot!

From: S. Wolfe swintrw@adl.com
To: Mr. N. Conti contifnd@secset.com

Mr. Conti,

Thank you for your kind offer of employment.

You will understand I find a proposal of this nature rather unusual, and I admit I'm at something of a loss to know how to respond.

If you furnish me with a little more information, it might possibly help me overcome my fear that this is an elaborate joke at my expense. Also, please, can you explain why you want a conservator and not a professional researcher?

Excuse my caution.

Yours,

Sara Wolfe

From: Mr. N. Conti contifnd@secset.com
To: Sara Wolfe swintrw@adl.com

Sara,

You are right to be cautious. I certainly have been, and I expect no less of you in return.

Later today you will receive an indication that any expense will fall on me. But till then please permit me to give you further information about the note-book's author.

The Reverend Bacon was an Englishman, a bookish curate, who studied European travelers in Asia during the Quattrocento. He stumbled on a number of references to my family's art collection, became intrigued, and set out to discover what happened to it. His research took him fifteen years, but eventually he established a fairly accurate catalogue of the collection that belonged to the merchant explorer Niccolo Dei Conti. He also chronicled the Conti family's failed attempts to keep the collection intact.

I am in the process of rebuilding that collection and cannot allow myself rest until I have reunited the pieces. Of the forty-two sculptures, I've re-acquired thirty-eight. The remaining four pieces elude me. If it were simply a question of money there would be no difficulty. The problem is one of discovery. I cannot buy what I cannot find. I want you to help me unearth these pieces. As I have said, I will pay you handsomely, but it is likely that acceptance of my proposal will lead to a far greater reward than money.

Even in its partial form the Reverend Bacon's history of the Conti collection is quite precise and as good as any account I might give. So I enclose some more pages from his damaged notebook (the Bacon vicarage was bombed during the Great War and only a fragment of his writings survived the subsequent fire), which I ask you to read receptively. I say that because you will see that Bacon came to believe the body of the collection had certain strange properties, including a capacity to alter those who embraced its spirit.

I understand, Sara, that to give up your safe job and ally yourself with a mysterious old man, whom you may never see, is asking a lot. However, I have enormous faith in your latent adventurousness.

Professional researchers are all well and good, but this is a task that requires a subtle sensibility that is both and neither academic or artistic.

I look forward to hearing from you.

Yours,

N. Conti

and the soul invested by Conti's wife Yasoda. These fourty-two figures, which the pair acquired during their travels, Niccolo protected with care until his death in April 1469. On inheriting his father's bequest, Umberto Conti bore the figures to Florence, but shortly thereafter, the newly crowned Pope Sixtus IV began to covet the collection and brought harsh means of persuasion down upon Umberto.

Umberto resisted manfully, but Sixtus would not be denied and redoubled his efforts with threats against Umberto's fledgling family. Cleverly, Umberto had the collection walled into his grandfather's wine cellar in the hillside town of Cortona and the Contis escaped northward to France. Mistakenly deducing that the collection had been spirited out of the country, Sixtus flew into one of the violent rages for which he was renowned and declared that he'd see Conti's head on a pike if he ever returned. Umberto never dared tread on holy soil again.

The collection rested silently within its makeshift tomb until 1532, when Elenore, Niccolo's granddaughter, returned to Florence to free it. She knew little of the collection other than that her grandfather and grandmother considered it to be possessed. Although a woman of natural sensibility, Elenore was unprepared for what she found and was overcome by the sight of the statues as they emerged one by one from the dimly lit cellar.

The erotic beauty of some of the objects bedazzled her and instantly she understood why Sixtus had shown such an interest in them. If he had been able to confiscate the collection as a heretical obscenity, he could then have placed it in his own extensive hoard of private sculpture, housed deep beneath the Vatican.

Elenore had the collection secretly transported to her home in France. When in 1535, she wed Philippe Hupert, it passed with her to her husband's family estate. The collection stayed safely cloistered in the Hupert house for 150 years. Then in 1685, a Papist fanatic named Giovanni Bollo spied the collection one night after the incumbent generation of Huperts had given him shelter from a vicious storm. He found the sculptures a vile affront to God's kingdom and vowed to his master to have the collection destroyed. Upon his return to Italy, he discovered Sixtus's document decreeing the Conte collection confiscan absente, and knowing that the Huperts would never willingly resign the collection, Bollo gathered a band of zealots and set forth to abduct the sculptures; his design is fired, and he and his band of brigands were caught in the act of theft and gleefully burnt to death by Hupert's diligent servants, who, being ardent Huguenots, could conceive no greater pleasure than dispatching the envoys of the Pope. After

Rajaram Jengke
Bhuvaneshvar

that fright, the three Hupert sisters, collective mistresses of the house, took it upon themselves to become guardians of the collection. To that end they divided it up, each taking fourteen sculptures to a seperate, safe destination.

The first sister, Marianne, took her portion of the collection to Amsterdam, where it remained until 1792 when it was purchased by a wealthy lace merchant who had acquired a taste for Eastern artifacts whilst trading in Indonesia. He kept the collection intact, as did his daughter; after her death in 1859, it was sold to an eccentric English actor who secreted the figures in his London townhouse for the specific purpose of shocking young lady visitors.

When he met his end at the hands of a jealous mistress, the sculptures were auctioned off. The collection's dissolution seemed imminent, but all the pieces were bought by Mrs. Coburn (a widow of high birth and tender beauty, who, to my heart's salvation, befriended me and gave me unlimited freedom to study the sculptures on condition that I do not make public her name, it being evident that possession of such art would occasion an irreparable scandal in polite society).

The second sister took her share of the collection to Egypt. She succeeded in keeping its existance secret from those who would damage it, as did her children. In 1750, the figures disappeared during a flood and were

...ned destroyed. However in 1888, all fourteen pieces turned up once more;: this time in the American capital, Washington, where they are kept to this day in the vault of a wealthy and stubborn American banker. My letters requesting a list of the collection's contents have been ignored, and I have sadly given up hope of ever seeing them.

The third sister did not fare so well. She kept the figures within French territory and found herself pursued once again by certain Romans. In a desperate attempt to keep the sculptures free from harm she had them buried in a deserted nunnery outside Marseilles. There they stayed until a cartograph showing their whereabouts came to the attention of one of Napoleon's swarming agents. In 1814 the agent dug up the sculptures and had them sent in a wagon to Paris. But while they were in transit the Corsican was defeated by Wellington at Waterloo, and all France dissolved into chaos. The abandoned wagon lay wasting in an old barn for a year until a returning soldier found them. He kept them, would not have them touched, told his neighbours that they were his booty brought home from the war in Spain. His sons were less sentimental, and one dark night when the old man lay deep in his cups, these unscrupulous wretches once again loaded the sculptures onto carts and returned them to Marseilles, where they sold them to the highest bidder at a makeshift portside sale. Bought by a variety of lascivious sea captains, Arab traders, and merchants, the sculptures were, in a single afternoon, cast forth into the world.

the separation of atoms of non-entity

Curiouser and curiouser.

What a fascinating prospect, dogging the Reverend's footsteps, hunting down these errant sculptures. An art gumshoe, traveling around, seeing unexpected places, smelling new air, eating different foods—it certainly would be a way of getting out of my rut.

Sara, you're being . . . What?

I'm being ridiculous. I'm letting my imagination run away with me. This is a fantasy. I'm falling for a trick of some kind.

Why do I let myself get so carried away? I have a good job at a museum. I was desperate to get that job—why would I give it up for some daydream that has probably been hatched by a crazy person?

But the Bacon notes are so alluring.

What do I do?

If I look up Niccolo Conti, I can at least establish whether Mr. Conti's ancestor actually existed or whether this is all an elaborate fabrication.

Found this in *Chamberlain's World Travelers and Explorers:*

NICCOLO DEI CONTI (1395–1469)
BORN IN CHIOGGIA, AN ITALIAN FISHING PORT NEAR VENICE. A MERCHANT WHO TRAVELED WIDELY IN ASIA AND JOURNEYED FOR 25 YEARS THROUGH EGYPT, PERSIA, INDIA, AND AS FAR EAST AS JAVA. MARRIED A WOMAN FROM DECCAN, A REGION OF INDIA, WHO BORE HIM FOUR CHILDREN BUT DIED, ALONG WITH TWO OF THE CHILDREN, FROM THE PLAGUE, IN CAIRO. WHILE TRAVELING, HE TRADED AND BUILT UP A SUBSTANTIAL COLLECTION OF ASIAN ART. RETURNED IN 1444 TO VENICE WHERE AN ACCOUNT OF HIS WANDERINGS WAS RECORDED BY THE POPE'S SCRIBE, POGGIO BRACCIOLINI. THE SCOPE OF CONTI'S JOURNEY AND THE QUALITY OF HIS ACCOUNT WERE UNMATCHED BY ANY OTHER FIFTEENTH-CENTURY TRAVELER.

Only partially edifying. At least it verifies Mr. Conti's story of his antecedent. What about Mr. Conti himself?

I don't believe this. A courier just turned up and asked me to sign for a delivery. I did so (assuming it was my supply of gold leaf from the Chicago art store). He started bringing boxes from a truck. I thought Oh no. I've ordered enough of the stuff to decorate the dome of a mosque.

The boxes contain a computer system. It must be worth thirty thousand dollars. It came with a note saying:

My computer is finding yours a bit antiquated.

This is a gift.

Accepting the job is not prerequisite.

    Yours,

    N. Conti

This is quite, quite bizarre.

From: S. Wolfe swintrw@adl.com
To: Mr. N. Conti contifnd@secset.com

Mr. Conti,

Thank you profusely, but I cannot accept your gift. Instead I will gladly look after the computer for as long as I'm in your employment.

    That is assuming we can agree on the salient details.

    Yours,

    Sara Wolfe

My God, I just did it. I accepted his job, just like that. Like I was putting the kettle on without thinking.

From: Mr. N. Conti contifnd@secset.com

To: Sara Wolfe swintrw@adl.com

Sara,

I'm so pleased you've decided to abet me in my search. If you wish to call it "looking after" the computer so be it. The important matter is that our systems are now in accord and we can work together rebuilding the collection.

Thank you.

N. Conti

Sara and I discussed her employment, and, as promised, I made her a highly generous offer. The amount was irrelevant, of course; it didn't matter to me if I paid her a hundred times that salary, but I had no wish to scare her away with an excessive sum.

I offered to provide her with an office-studio but she said she would prefer to work from home. At first she was resistant to the idea of conducting all business by computer, but eventually she agreed that it was in the spirit of the twenty-first century. If only she knew how ironic it was that I of all people should be making that argument.

I will not bore you with accounts of organizational fine detail. Suffice to say, Sara accepted my proposal and became my much-needed assistant.

My first request was that she should spend a few hours researching Hindu mythology, particularly the deities Shiva and Parvati, Ganesha, and Kali. Once she has done that I will give her the list of the four missing sculptures. I have indicated that her job will require her to do the best she can to find them. I shall not tell her that it is unlikely that she will find anything about the sculptures I do not already know, but it is important she be grounded in the subject matter.

 PAGE 533. SARA. COMPUTER DIARY

Mr. Conti has given me my opening task.

It's the first time since I was beginning college that going to the library feels like an adventure.

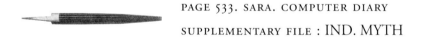 PAGE 533. SARA. COMPUTER DIARY

SUPPLEMENTARY FILE : IND. MYTH

Every book gave me different versions of these stories. Very confusing. When characters are reincarnated, their names change—I think. For example: Devi the great mother is at times Sati or Parvati or Durga or Kali.

From what I can understand, these stories, which on the surface are about gods, demons, feuding, anger, revenge, love and other dramas, are really a way of alluding to the notion of universal paradox.

SATI BECOMING PARVATI

Sati's father, Daksha, and Shiva, Sati's husband, were not on
good terms. Daksha held a big sacrificial party and invited
all the Gods except Shiva. Sati was angry at this insult to her
husband and went to her father's house to complain. Shiva
was pleased at her loyalty but counseled her to hold her temper.
When she arrived her father mocked her and her husband. Because she
had promised Shiva she would not strike Daksha and because her rage
knew no limits, she immolated herself on the sacrificial fire. Shiva, furi-
ous and tormented by the loss of his beloved wife, sent a demon to
destroy everyone at the ceremony. However, Vishnu interceded and Shiva
relented and brought the guests back to life. He then went into deep med-
itation to wait for Sati to be reincarnated, which she eventually was, in the form of Parvati.

GANESHA'S ELEPHANT HEAD

Parvati was lonely because Shiva had been away for many years, so she made
herself a chubby little boy out of clay and brought him to life. One day while
Parvati was bathing, Shiva returned. Not recognizing Shiva and wishing to protect his mother, the boy, Ganesha, tried to stop Shiva from going near the
pool. Shiva was unused to resistance and without thinking lopped off
the boy's head. Parvati was heartbroken so Shiva sent a bunch of goblins
to find a replacement head. They couldn't find anything suitable but,
rather than return with nothing, brought back a baby elephant head. Shiva
didn't hold out much hope of it appeasing Parvati but placed it on the child's
body anyway. Much to Shiva's amazement, when he brought the child back to
life, Parvati was delighted with her son's new appearance.

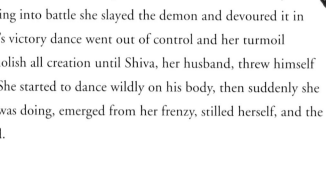

A wicked monster was ravaging the world, and it seemed inevitable that all would be lost unless the gods summoned Kali to destroy the creature. Leaping into battle she slayed the demon and devoured it in a single gulp. Kali's victory dance went out of control and her turmoil threatened to demolish all creation until Shiva, her husband, threw himself down before her. She started to dance wildly on his body, then suddenly she realized what she was doing, emerged from her frenzy, stilled herself, and the universe was saved.

 PAGE 534. SARA. COMPUTER DIARY

A fortune in my account and I haven't started working full time yet! But as Mr. Conti pointed out, if he didn't guarantee me one year's income I would have no incentive to find his family's sculptures speedily. Still—so much money in one shot. I want to tell someone about my incredible windfall, but I guess it's better that I keep it to myself.

Since the cat incident I keep finding myself looking in Marco's direction. He's got a way of moving that's very smooth, without stops and starts. This afternoon he was standing near me, talking to one of the assistant curators, when I noticed the diffused sunlight shining through the amber hairs on the back of his neck. I must have been thinking *cat* because I caught myself just starting to reach out and stroke him. Disconcerting in the extreme! But I really would have liked to get to know him. Bit late now.

Christine came over this evening. I said something—I can't remember what—and she said I was being indirect, that I always sounded a bit like I'd swallowed an old book.

"How do you mean," I said.

She said, "You have a funny way of speaking. Don't get me wrong, it's not that I don't like it—it's very you. It's just sort of formal."

It's true, I do like words. Words that slow things down—give me time. I suppose I use them as protection. At times it must seem elongated and overly elaborate. (Is that an example? Could I have said something like long-winded?)

Damn you, Christine, you've got me analyzing my own language now.

After we'd drunk half a bottle of wine I weakened and told her about the job and Mr. Conti. She said she could see I was getting restless at the museum and it didn't surprise her that I'd decided to quit. She said she was glad for me, but her tone wasn't exactly convincing and I realized she was upset. It's hard to believe, but I think she needs me around. For all her bravado, she is as lonely and untrusting of the world as I am. We face the same fears in opposite ways. It dawned on me that that's probably why we get along. I was still musing over this rather obvious insight when the name Blake cut into my consciousness. Christine had changed subjects and was telling me about Blake, her latest boyfriend, and how she liked to walk behind him so that she could (and I quote) watch his ass swing. I was still wondering what route she'd taken to get from my new employment to Blake's butt when she moved on to try and entice me to go out with Blake's best friend Murray.

I said I'd never been on a blind date and had no intention of starting now, thank you very much.

She told me I was emotionally constipated. (Only Christine could say something like that and nearly get away with it. I knew she was getting back at me for deserting her and the museum.)

I told her I was not constipated emotionally or otherwise. I said I hated set-ups and any man who wanted one wasn't of any interest to me. I know I sounded pompous, but she was really getting under my skin.

She said I was stuck-up, because I was the only twenty-six-year-old virgin in California. She knows it's not true. I wish I'd never told her about Stephen. She began pontificating about how a lot of people have lousy experiences the first time but they pick themselves up and try again.

What does she know? It's not her who wakes up in the night still trying to fight Stephen off. It's not her who wants to vomit every time she thinks about the humiliation.

I told her I didn't want to hear any more, but she just said "Phooey" and went on saying how I was scared stiff of disappointment or failure or something. And then, guessing she might have gone a bit far, she switched to trying to make me laugh by retelling the story of her date with the TV soap star and his pet snake. But I wasn't really listening by then. I'd drifted into reliving an experience of my own. I was standing in front of the drawing of the Shiva—feeling the exquisite stroke of his hands running their traces across my bare skin.

GUARD AGAINST SIDE-SLIP

From: Mr. N. Conti contifnd@secset.com

To: Sara Wolfe swintrw@adl.com

Sara,

The four pieces still to be found are as follows (heights approximate):

Dancing Ganesha, eighth century, Uttar Pradesh (48")

A Celestial Woman under flowering branch, tenth century (30")

Kali, twelfth century, Cochin (12")

Parvati, thirteenth century, South India (27")

Please start searching for all known examples that fit these descriptions.

N. Conti

 From: S. Wolfe swintrw@adl.com

To: Mr. N. Conti contifnd@secset.com

Mr. Conti,

I have received the list and will begin my search.

It would be helpful if I knew how you contrived to track down the thirty-eight figures already in your possession, if only to give me an idea of the magnitude of my task.

Also, can you tell me what you know about Niccolo Conti himself? The information I've gathered so far is minimal.

Sara

From: Mr. N. Conti contifnd@secset.com

To: Sara Wolfe swintrw@adl.com

Sara,

Bacon's notes were remarkably accurate.

Fortunately for me the two main groups of fourteen figures were kept intact.

The first set was bequeathed to Bacon himself, by Mrs. Coburn. Late in his life he had them put into storage while he considered their fate. But a massive stroke robbed him of his decision, and the bank that had been told to settle the storage company's invoices until instructed otherwise continued to do so over half a decade. When the storage company went bankrupt I came across a local newspaper article describing how various items including the Reverend Bacon's unopened boxes were in the hands of the bailiffs. I immediately guessed that the boxes contained my sculptures. I contacted the receiver and settled on a price for the sale of the warehouse and its contents. My instinct was, to my enormous satisfaction, correct.

The second group came on the market through a private dealer in New Hampshire in 1981. The negotiations were difficult as there were many collectors who showed an interest in purchasing the sculptures. The dealer was prepared to sell me nine of the figures but wanted the other five to be bought by a major museum to enhance his standing as a leading antiquarian. In the end, I convinced him otherwise: I matched the museum's price and let him know of a rumor I'd heard concerning a clandestine arrangement he had with his wife's younger sister.

He judiciously chose my offer.

The fourteen figures that were sold on the Marseilles dock have been infinitely harder to track down. Bacon was correct in deducing that the individual pieces traveled far and wide. A detailed account of my search for them would fill a heavy tome. Four figures were in private hands—getting them was a matter of money and timing. Five were in museums spread throughout the world. These were more difficult. Curators are often more clutchingly acquisitive than private collectors so I had to allow them to trade up for more prestigious items. In one case, I had to offer half the contents of a Viking burial mound before a particularly rapacious curator would part with my Bronze Krishna.

The tenth of the Marseilles pieces and the thirty-eighth overall, a Vishnu Boar, turned up in a Hollywood studio lot sale. It was presumed to be a copy, but it very definitely wasn't. How it got there is a mystery.

One of the four remaining figures, the Celestial Woman, is coming up for auction shortly. I'll keep you informed.

The other three are as yet undetected. As you will see, with patience, there is always a way of acquiring a work—it's locating it that is the problem.

I look forward to having your competent help in that matter.

N. Conti

I *was, of course, not being fully honest here. The situation was in fact reversed. I expected to be able to establish their location myself. Sara's role was to be the securing and taking possession of the figures. However, the mild deception was not, as you might think, a purely selfish act; it was also designed for Sara's sake.*

Awoke at four-thirty. Clearly my lack of money worries is not going to improve my sleep pattern.

Seems a bit early to be nostalgic about the museum, especially as yesterday was my last day, but I'm missing the place already. The mustiness, the light pouring in through the lovely high windows, the infuriating gurgling coming from the ancient plumbing system, sketching in quiet corners when there's a lull, Christine (sometimes), the Shiva, and Marco.

I really blew it by not overcoming my shyness with Marco. I like him a lot. When he said good-bye to me he shook my hand with great gentleness, like it was a delicate paw.

From: Mr. N. Conti contifnd@secset.com

To: Sara Wolfe swintrw@adl.com

Sara,

Have a look at the catalogue that's going to come up on your screen.

It's from a small gallery in New Orleans.

I've indicated the significant area in the relevant painting. I can't be certain, but this could be my Ganesha.

I'd like you to go to New Orleans and see the painter, Alexander Lorac. I understand he lives only a few houses from the Simenon. Find out where he obtained those Ganesha images.

I've booked your flight for 2:30 tomorrow afternoon. You can pick up your tickets from the United desk at S.F. Airport.

Expenses all covered, have fun.

N. Conti

SIMENON GALLERY

ALEXANDER LORAC

RECENT WORKS

Alexander Lorac's work juxtaposes the amorphous colors of the Indian sub-continent with the tactile roughness of its ephemeral cultural remains. Even though he has never visited Asia, Lorac's vision has enabled him to create a world suffused in the light of his own mind's eye.

SIMENON GALLERY

467 Jackson Avenue

New Orleans, Louisiana

Me flying first class—how satisfyingly decadent.

Kept sneaking furtive looks at the other first-class passengers, trying to guess whether they'd paid all that extra money themselves or if they were, like me, traveling at someone else's expense.

Took a taxi to the Simenon Gallery, an ornate green and ocher shopfront that was a little too prissy for my taste. While I was waiting to see if they'd give me Lorac's address, I looked around the exhibition. Liked the pictures a lot—rich, timeless, and not even remotely prissy; they made me want to tumble into them and delve around.

After ten minutes or so the tight-faced receptionist-cum-salesperson gave me Lorac's address, which, as Mr. Conti had suggested, was just down the street.

Alexander Lorac was waiting for me, leaning in his studio doorway. He was an overly relaxed and good-looking young man in a loose white cotton shirt and maroon waistcoat. I remember thinking Damn! I'd have preferred you old and leathery. His face wore an expression halfway between a smile and a smirk. He greeted me with the news that the gallery had called to remind him politely that they were entitled to 33% on all private sales during the period of the show, and by the way, should they send me over? He said, "It's just canned soup to them."

I asked him if he minded their lack of trust.

He said, "It works both ways. What they are unaware of won't hurt them."

I felt slightly uncomfortable and tried to explain that as much as I liked his pictures I wasn't there to buy one. I quickly produced Mr. Conti's annotated catalogue and told Lorac that I was searching for an eighth-century Ganesha that looked like the one in his picture. I was talking rapidly, half expecting him to tell me to go away, but he didn't. In fact, his smile changed from predatory to something quite genuine.

"Wait here," he said, and stepping back, disappeared into the darkness of his studio. Seconds later he came out with a little elephant figure. It was a Ganesha but only a quarter of the size of the one I was after. He said, "I don't think this is what you're looking for—it's not an original."

I must have looked quite crestfallen because he apologized for disappointing me.

I assured him with as much professionalism as I could muster that it certainly wasn't his fault, but the wind had gone out of my sails. I wanted, so badly, to return in triumph with the Ganesha under my arm.

When Lorac found out how far I'd come, he insisted on inviting me in for a tour of his studio as recompense. The studio's main room took me by surprise—New Orleans disappeared. In its place a flaking blue and rose ceiling capped four high walls whose surfaces were covered from top to bottom in a vast mural that merged an earthy red and green Indian landscape with a great mass of collaged ephemera, including everything from old postcards and yellowing train tickets to scraps from Punjabi newspapers. The mural was overwhelming, but it was only the first layer of visual assault—hanging directly on top of the painted stucco were Lorac's framed paintings and drawings, and set into the wall were a number of alcoves and niches that held within their shadows carvings and sculptures. The effect was one of depth upon depth and illusion upon illusion. The density of imagery was making my eyes ache and I rubbed them vigorously. The overt sensuousness of the room made me very self-conscious. To compensate, I did what I always do when I'm flustered—I asked questions. I asked him how he came to be interested in the art of India, and if the mural was his doing.

He replied that the work was his and that when he was in his last year at art college his tutors had told him he needed to find a subject to get obsessive about. He picked India because it was as far away from his cultural experience as he could imagine and therefore had the best potential for inspiring his struggling imagination. It had been ten years since he left school, and he said he was still barely scratching the surface of his chosen obsession.

We talked for a fascinating hour, and then, as I was leaving, I found myself asking if he'd consider selling me his Ganesha statue. Without realizing it, I'd begun to want to own the chubby little elephant.

He said, "No, I couldn't. It's a talisman. My girlfriend gave it to me the day we met, and even though it sounds sentimental and over-dramatic, I know she won't leave me as long as I look after our friend."

I said of course I understood that, but did he maybe have a photograph of it?

"Sorry," he said, and then after a moment's thought, retreated into a back room. He returned clutching a small oil painting of the elephant boy.

"Here, have this," he said.

"How much do you want for it?" I asked with caution.

"It's yours," he replied, smiling. "Remember? The gallery said I wasn't to sell you anything. Anyway, Ganesha has provided for me, and what goes around should come around."

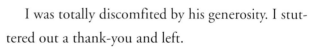

I was totally discomfited by his generosity. I stuttered out a thank-you and left.

It was only later that I realized he'd given me something to show Mr. Conti. If I wasn't coming back with the missing Ganesha, at least I had a recognizable facsimile.

I decided not to stay in New Orleans but return to San Francisco that evening, using the open ticket that had been provided for me. Killed an hour, before heading to the airport, in an antique store, where I bought a snake

charmer card to remind me how misleading appearances can be.

Why didn't I stay on? I suppose it was partly a desire to run home to my apartment and put the Ganesha painting in the place I'd mentally reserved for it, and partly because the thought of stopping overnight unnerved me. I'm being chicken, I know, but the idea of eating in a restaurant or going to a movie by myself, exposed as an unattached person in a strange city, feels far too daunting.

From: S. Wolfe swintrw@adl.com
To: Mr. N. Conti contifnd@secset.com

Mr. Conti,

Lorac owns a Ganesha figure, but it's only a quarter-sized copy (nineteenth century, I think).

Transmitting a Lorac painting of same—can you confirm that the original full-sized version of this piece is the one we're looking for?

Sara

From: Mr. N. Conti contifnd@secset.com

To: Sara Wolfe swintrw@adl.com

Sara,

The painter has indulged in a fair degree of poetic license, but the figure's stance is unmistakable. I have no doubt the copy was based on my Ganesha.

Quarter-size, you say. Interesting.

Sorry your trip wasn't fully successful, but you've made good progress.

N. Conti

PAGE 536. SARA. COMPUTER DIARY

Found an old black frame that fits the Ganesha painting perfectly. I've hung it in my bedroom between the dresser and the Paul Strand photo. Funny, the figure on the far right of that photo reminds me of Alexander Lorac. Just did a sketch of it. Strand's man is Italian and rural, but something in the way he's standing—don't know, maybe it's just that the waistcoat's the same.

Anyway, Ganesha looks at home.

Tomorrow I must write and thank Alexander Lorac properly.

Suddenly I'm being given presents, and for once it doesn't make me feel ashamed.

Why?

Am I changing?

From: Mr. N. Conti contifnd@secset.com

To: Sara Wolfe swintrw@adl.com

Sara,

The Celestial Woman is coming up for auction in New York next week.
I'd like you to attend and bid on my behalf. I could manage electronically as I've
done in the past, but I would feel much more comfortable if you were there to
be my eyes and ears. The bidding may become excessive. That's not a problem.
Don't lose your nerve; we have unlimited funds. All I ask is that you secure the
figure and watch carefully those bidding against us. Now that I'm this close,
there may well be obstructions.

Here's the relevant page from the auction catalogue. Our prize is lot 122.

To help you get the feel of the current market I'm putting you on a network
that gives access to all the catalogues and prices realized at the major auction
houses throughout the world in the last ten years.

N. Conti

LOT 120

Bronze Tibetan monastery bell

16th century, southern Tibet

Height: 34 cm

One of the earliest examples of Buddhist prayer bells to come to the West. Small as these types of bells are, their powers of resonance are remarkable; they could be heard for 20 or 30 miles across the clear air of rural Tibet.

LOT 121

Collection of Indian miniature figures

This unique collection of many thousands of miniatures was assembled over a period of 50 years by the late Major Thomas Doyle. The diminutive ivory, wood, clay, and plaster figures depict every aspect of Indian life. The collection begins with 39 17th-century chess pieces and ends with 273 post-Independence children's toy figurines.

LOT 122

Sandstone figure of a Celestial woman beneath a blooming bush

11th century, central-western India

Height: 73 cm

This splendid Shivan maiden almost certainly came from Madhya Pradesh and was probably a temple's porch-hole bracket. It is not unlike another that faces in the opposite direction, whose origin has been attributed to Surwaya. Her face is very finely carved and her body has a smooth voluptuousness that sets the sculpture apart from the more roughly hewn sandstone figures of the period.

From: S. Wolfe swintrw@adl.com
To: Mr. N. Conti contifnd@secset.com

Mr. Conti,

I don't wish to sound faint hearted, but I'm afraid I've never bid at an auction, let alone one of this importance. Are you sure you want to put the responsibility in my hands?

    Sara

From: Mr. N. Conti contifnd@secset.com
To: Sara Wolfe swintrw@adl.com

Sara,

Absolutely!

There's an antique auction in San Francisco this week at Butterfield's, on San Bruno Avenue. Why don't you go and practice? Bid on something you like—see what you can buy for $500 dollars. The Conti Foundation will pay for it.

There's nothing like experience to obliterate stage fright.

N. Conti

PAGE 541. SARA. COMPUTER DIARY

I've taken to greeting the Ganesha painting when I walk in the room. Whenever I look at him he seems to radiate bounce. Is that right, can something radiate bounce? Anyway, I know what I mean. He makes everything in my bedroom, including me, appear more vibrant.

It's a coincidence, no doubt, but I've been sleeping much better ever since I got him. This morning I didn't wake till six. I still leapt out of bed like I'd been fired from a cannon, but that's nothing new.

For no reason (?) I remembered the first time Mum and Dad let me drink—alcohol, I mean. It was a Sunday and we'd driven out of the city and up into Napa Valley to visit the Farrolls, Mom's boss, his wife, and their daughter Stephanie, who was about my age. We had lunch at a big round table in their garden, there was the hum of bees everywhere, and Stephanie and I were given huge glasses containing a full half-inch of red wine.

I looked at Dad, and he nodded his approval. I looked at Stephanie, and she grinned and raised her eyebrows. I sipped with apprehension and expectation, and it tasted incredibly strong. I felt enormously grown up—considerably more so than I do now.

PAGE 542. SARA. COMPUTER DIARY

Had enormous fun at Butterfield's auction. My heart was pounding when I started to bid on a folder of architectural engravings. I was sure I was going to get it with my final bid of $380, but then somebody new jumped in, and I watched it slip from my grasp. It eventually fetched $650, which was a relief because if it had sold for $420 I might have been kicking myself.

I decided I really wanted the miniature black corner cabinet, but that skyrocketed and went for more than $800. Then came the beetle collection in a worn bamboo box—like rows of school children sleeping in a dormitory. They were marvelous and I didn't think I stood a hope of getting them, and nearly missed my chance. I still can't believe I have them for only $140.

With my remaining $360 I bought a beautiful set of nineteenth-century encyclopedias, full of illustrations that I can scan into the computer and use with my diary entries.

If I feel like this about stuff in the $100 range, what's it going to be like when I'm bidding tens of thousands?

I took this job to have new experiences—can't complain now that I'm getting them.

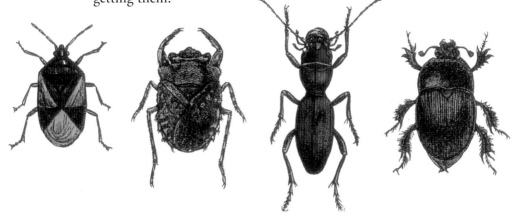

 PAGE 544. SARA. COMPUTER DIARY

Went to Delato's (diabolical) Deli around twelve-thirty. Marco was there waiting in line for a sandwich. I didn't give myself time to think; I simply walked up to him and said, "Hi, Marco."

We talked. We actually talked. Once we got going it was pretty easy, really. I didn't stutter or burble and on one occasion there was even a hint of lingering eye contact. After a few minutes he had to get back to work. But I didn't mind because I was positively glowing. I still am.

Have to pack for New York. Think I'll take my Ganesha for company.

Been thinking about Alexander Lorac's collages. I want to see
if I can make images like that—ones that aren't as tight as
my regular little diary icons.

Not bad, but it's a bit dour considering my elated state.
Must buy some more rubber stamps.

Decided to go straight to the Marion auction house's viewing room to see the Celestial Woman. She was utterly beautiful. Looking at her, I felt an indescribable sense of longing. The nobility of her sensuality made a mockery of our buying and selling. She was uninhibited, un-coy, devoid of the polarities of calculated innocence and hedonistic sin that dominate female figures in so much Western art (Phew, I sound like I'm writing for *Art International*).

Found myself doing a strange thing. The sort of thing that I would normally consider new-age gibberish. I asked her, under my breath, if she would allow me to take her back to Mr. Conti. As soon as I'd done it I was sort of embarrassed. I thought, first the Shiva drawing and now this. I'm unraveling.

A few seconds later I had a sense that I was being watched and I half-turned to see a man staring at me. I wondered for a second if it was Mr. Conti, but then I realized this person was humorless and only middle-aged. He was dressed in an expensive-looking charcoal gray suit and a powder blue cashmere turtleneck, and he sported a neatly clipped beard, but neither his facial hair nor the wool around his throat could disguise the fact that he was quite chinless.

When I faced him his gaze stayed on me. Sizing me up, appraising me, not as a woman but as a competitor. Then his eyes flashed away, and I saw I had been dismissed as a person of no consequence.

I thought, Right. I'll show you. Just wait till tomorrow.

My hotel was so swanky it had no name on the outside of the building, but the taxi driver knew it anyway. He warned me that everyone wore black there. He was right. I couldn't tell who were the staff and who were the guests. I considered putting on my black slacks and sweater to see if I could pick up a few tips.

As I was waiting to register, I read their brochure: ". . . and the lobby combines vaulting primary triangles and sumptuous wide-bellied columns in a stylish Postmodernism." I could see the triangles, though the stylish bit was beyond me, and the term *Postmodernism* has always seemed to me rather silly.

My bedroom was Neo-Dada poky.

I know, I'm being cynical—it's New York; it's too hard-edged for me. I couldn't sleep. Someone was hurling trash cans up and down the side street all night. At three I finally gave up and read. Dropped off around the time I normally wake, came to at eight, far from bright-eyed and bushy-tailed.

The auction room was just how I'd pictured it—voluminous, gilt-ridden and stuffed to the rafters with well-heeled folk who gave the impression of knowing exactly what they were doing. Reminded myself to watch everyone else. Made mental notes of their mannerisms to distract myself from panicking totally. Noticed I was the only woman in the room not wearing makeup. That didn't help.

Took a back seat, so I could see everything that was going on. The row filled quickly, except for a seat five or six to my right. Then the auction began. The lots came up and were knocked down at a staggering pace. On television, they only show the staged parts of the auction where everything is slowed down for the twenty-million-dollar sale of the Van Gogh or whatever. Here it was happening so quickly it was often difficult to see who was bidding. Sometimes I'd see an impatient signal, but mostly it seemed to be catalogue twitchers battling against the auction house phone staff. Gradually, I got a feel for it.

Around Lot 100, I noticed the chinless man take the vacant seat at the end of the row. He didn't look my way, just stared fixedly ahead, giving me his cheese wedge profile. I knew for certain he was going to be bidding against me for the Celestial Woman.

When Lot 122 was brought in, in the embrace of a porter, the room became almost quiet. Only the Chihuahua clasped to the breast of the bejeweled purple rinse three rows in front of me seemed oblivious to the Celestial Woman.

I knew that I wasn't meant to bid early, but I was scared the whole thing might be over before I blinked, so I sat very still, concentrating, listening for the bidding to falter. I didn't have to worry. When the early bidders were reduced to one, the auctioneer looked over at Chinless, who almost imperceptibly nodded his head. There was another staccato sequence of bids ending with the auctioneer looking toward the unseen bidder near the front. It was at this point that my hand decided to lift itself. I don't mean that it was anything supernatural; it was just that I was so tense my arm felt separated from my body when I started to move it. I could feel Chinless turn my way. He bid again. I kept my hand up. He bid again. I kept my hand up. I watched him out of the corner of my eye. He tried again. I didn't move. He was becoming agitated. He looked over to the wall on his right. Standing very erect and half-hidden in the folds of a dark red curtain was a priest who was talking urgently into a cellular phone. The priest looked up and nodded in the direction of Chinless. Chinless bid again. My hand stayed aloft. I closed my ears to the huge sums of money the auctioneer was by then barely able to avoid salivating over. I hoped that when Mr. Conti said "no limit," he meant it. Finally the priest flicked the phone closed and shook his head. Chinless in turn shook his head at the auctioneer and the lot was knocked down to the Conti Foundation.

That surprised me enormously because it meant the auctioneer knew who I was all along. Not so Chinless; he winced when he heard who had outbid him, and I distinctly saw him mouth "Niccolo" at the priest. As I was leaving the auction room I noticed the two of them locked in a very animated conversation.

After the auction I was too busy wallowing in my victory to pay much attention to the chinless man and the priest. (I had no idea I was *that* competitive.) Now the thought of them makes me uncomfortable. What were they doing there? Why did they want the Celestial Woman so badly? When Chinless mouthed the name Niccolo, was he referring to the original Conti or could it be that Mr. Conti has the same name as his ancestor?

Need to find out more about the original Niccolo, get some more background, know what he was like. I could ask Mr. Conti again, but I don't want to appear pushy, in case he's forgotten or for some reason doesn't want to answer. Hmm. Think I'll try Uncle Peter—see what he can dig up at his beloved university.

T he security cameras were positioned well enough for me to see quite adequately, and I was very impressed by Sara's handling of the auction. She dealt with the holy opposition most convincingly. The reserve bid I left with the Marion was, I promise, only a safety net.

From: Peter Carroll: pcexlib@dabis.com

To: Sara Wolfe: swintrw@adl.com

Hello Sara,

How are you, my sweet? It's been a long time.

I won't say anything like "I can hardly believe that you're twenty-six" because although I'm thinking it, it leads me to consider my antiquity and, worse, my *mortality.*

Seeing that you are undoubtedly a busy person (at your age, I was excessively so), I'll dive in and respond to your request.

I'd never heard of Niccolo Dei Conti, but he certainly turns out to be an interesting character. One of those odd people who are so ahead of their own century that History doesn't know what to make of them. The extent of his travels was staggering.

As per instructions, I'm glossing over encyclopedic references in favor of a more obscure source. I found a book called Pero Tafur: Travels and Adventures *(copy of cover enclosed), which is an 1874 translation of a Spanish book. Which in turn comes from a ninety-one-and-a-half folio manuscript written in the middle of the fifteenth century by said Pero Tafur, a Spanish trader. They won't let me scan the inside of the book because they say the spine is fragile, so you'll have to put up with the tasters I'm picking out for you. If nothing else it confirms fairly conclusively Niccolo Conti's credibility as an explorer.*

I will avoid my tendency toward scholarly (cough) circumnavigation and, as they say in the vernacular, cut to the chase.

On page 84 Tafur begins the account of his chance meeting with Conti:

"I went to the shore of the Red Sea, which is half a league from Mount Sinai [either Pero or the translator had big trouble with distances] to see the arrival of the caravan, and I found that a Venetian had come with it, called Niccolo de' Conti [this is our man—as you know spelling was less pedantic back

THE BROADWAY TRAVELLERS

EDITED BY SIR E. DENISON ROSS
AND EILEEN POWER

PERO TAFUR

TRAVELS AND
ADVENTURES
1435–1439

Translated and Edited with an
Introduction by Malcolm Letts

GEORGE ROUTLEDGE & SONS, LTD.

then], a gentleman of good birth who brought with him his native wife, she being said to be a sorceress, and two sons and two daughters, all of whom had become Moors, having been forced to renounce their faith in Mecca, which is the Moors' Holy place."

After Conti and Tafur met, Conti agreed to relate the story of his travels. They were both merchants, but the similarities ended there. I get the distinct impression that Conti was in a different league from Tafur—more sophisticated, a lot smarter. I think he was playing with the younger and more credulous Tafur when he told his tale. I have no doubt Conti journeyed where he said he did, but he added a little color to make the telling more interesting.

The first part of Conti's story, which deals with his changing fortune:

". . . at the time when Timur-Beg was ruling I found myself in Alexandria with certain moneys of my father, and from there I had to go to Babylonia, and through bad management and youthful inexperience, for I was only eighteen years of age, I lost what I had, and as I was desperate and ashamed to return home, I went to the place where Timur-Beg was, and remained a year at his court. From there I sought the means to go into Greater India and learnt that all was secure [I presume he meant that law and order prevailed], for at that time the rule of Timur-Beg extended from India to the Red Sea. When I arrived in India I was taken to see Prester John [Prester was a name bestowed on the mighty Christian monarchs of Asia], who received me very graciously and showed me many favors . . . I gained much wealth."

Further on Conti moves on and gives Tafur a taste of The Wonders of the East:

". . . in that mountain of Ceylon very fine cinnamon is grown . . . there is a fruit tree there, like a great ripe pumpkin, inside it are three separate fruits, each having its own taste . . . a sea coast where the crabs, on reaching the land, and being exposed to the air, turn to stone.

"I've seen people eating human flesh . . . this be it understood, is a heathen

practice . . . Christians eating the raw flesh of animals, after which it is necessary to eat of a very odoriferous herb within fifteen to twenty days, but if they delay longer they become lepers. [social, of course]

". . . monsters in human shape, such as some have reported, that is men with one leg and one eye, or but a cubit in height, or as tall as a lance . . . I have never met with such, but I've seen beasts with very strange shapes . . . an elephant of great size and as white as snow, which is a very strange thing, since they are almost all black . . . also an ass not much larger than a hound, and of as many colors as it is possible to enumerate: also many unicorns and other animals, which it would take too long to describe."

He continues most ingeniously mixing fact and fiction for twelve pages but I'll go no further as I'm sure you have the gist. Conti makes no reference to a collection of artifacts, but that's hardly surprising. Transporting them would have been a highly dodgy exercise and Conti would be unlikely to boast of it to Tafur.

And you say you're working for his descendant who's looking for Conti's lost treasures.

That's the sort of job I've been wanting all my life. You lucky minx.

Oh well! I'd probably only get homesick for my books.

Hope these tidbits are passably stimulating.

All my best to your mother.

As ever, your succinct servant,

Peter Carrol

From: S. Wolfe swintrw@adl.com
To: Mr. N. Conti contifnd@secset.com

Mr. Conti,

My uncle has sent me a short sampling of *Pero Tafur: Travels and Adventures.*
Do you by any chance have a copy of the book—if so, could I borrow it?

Sara

From: Mr. N. Conti contifnd@secset.com
To: Sara Wolfe swintrw@adl.com

Sara,

I wouldn't bother with Tafur. He was no more than a child when Conti met him
and was inclined to miss the jest.

If you want to know about Conti's travels, you could try reading scribe
Poggio's version for Pope Eugene, but I warn you, it's a brutalization. The classical
Latin combined with Poggio's political expedience has seriously corrupted the
subject matter.

Leave this with me, and I'll write you a more accessible account.

N. Conti

Mr. Conti speaks so authoritatively. How does he know this stuff? I need to find out more. There's things going on here I don't understand.

I hate being kept in the dark.

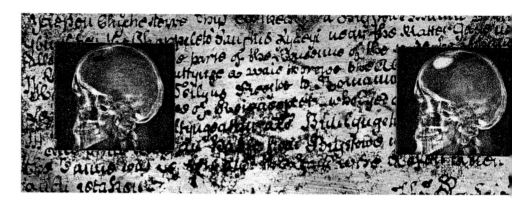

 From: S. Wolfe swintrw@adl.com
To: Mr. N. Conti contifnd@secset.com

Mr. Conti,

I hope you won't be offended by this, but my experience at the auction leads me to feel that I'm getting involved in events more complicated than a simple hunt for Indian sculpture.

I've shied away from asking you direct questions, but now I must. Am I becoming entangled in anything I wouldn't want to?

Sara

From: Mr. N. Conti contifnd@secset.com

To: Sara Wolfe swintrw@adl.com

Sara,

Do you mean illegal? No.

Do you mean dangerous? Not for you. You're protected far beyond your comprehension.

You are right, though. This is not a simple hunt for art.

At the moment, there is much that I cannot tell you, as events have yet to unwind. However, I can tell you one thing, and there being no easy way to reduce the peculiarity of what I am about to relate, I will be forthright: Niccolo Dei Conti is not my ancestor. I am his ghost, the ghost of Niccolo Dei Conti.

Ghost is a very broad term and although I have met no others of my ilk, I am assuming that is what I am.

Niccolo Conti

From: S. Wolfe swintrw@adl.com

To: Mr. N. Conti contifnd@secset.com

Mr. Conti,

You are kidding me, aren't you?

This is a joke, right?

Sara

From: Mr. N. Conti contifnd@secset.com

To: Sara Wolfe swintrw@adl.com

Sara,

No. This is no joke. I'm deadly serious.

After I was struck down by lightning back in 1469, I found myself drifting aimlessly without a real comprehension of time. I was neither in nor out of the physical world; I had no memory, only a vague consciousness that took succor from any source of electricity I came upon.

One day I encountered a new conductor and became hypnotized by the vibrating electrical pulses. I tried to get closer to the charge—I pressed myself toward the heart of the glow, and, without warning, I became saturated with light. My memory returned, and I was again Niccolo Conti: I could think, I could move, and yet I had no body. I could travel in lines, forward or backward. Voices passed through me. I could hear, but I could not understand. I was trapped inside the telephone wires. I tried to escape, fleeing this way and that, to no avail. I was a prisoner, or so I thought at first.

Slowly, I learned. Slowly, I learned new languages, learned to ride the wires, listen to conversations, gather knowledge. Years passed. Then, on a spring evening in 1930, I heard two professors of unspecified origins, speaking in broken English about an Indian sculpture. The conversation began, "The mark on the nape of the neck of the Gwalior Visnu, it is interesting, is it not?" The other replied, "Not Asian: perhaps ownership identification placed there by European collector." I listened intently, and, from the ensuing dialogue, I became certain I was listening to a description of one of the figures from my collection. It dawned on me that I could use the wires to track down my whole collection, and at that moment I understood what my wife had been trying to tell me. For years, as she and I had gathered the figures she would say to me, "When we part, you must bring them together again." She could always see further ahead than I.

Initially it was hard trying to find my way around. I wasn't omnipresent, and traveling the wires, although quick, wasn't instant. For years I did little more than listen, but at least I listened with a purpose. Then I discovered the existence of Bacon's notebook while I was eavesdropping on an antiquarian bookseller who was laboriously listing his latest acquisitions to a prospective client. Bacon was an enormous boon for me.

I pinpointed some of the sculptures' whereabouts, but it was a laborious task that offered no real hope of gaining control over the objects I wanted so badly. Then, to my salvation, telephone lines became linked to computers and everything changed. My day had come, and all began to be possible. I merely had to master the labyrinth in order to realize my dream.

The first step was financing. That was easy: with the privilege of inside information, making a vast fortune on the stock markets was child's play. Transmitting messages, moving money, instructing couriers, all were easy and I soon had the power I required.

Now I am close to regaining all that was lost. But I am confined in this electric cage, and I need your help. Will you continue to work with me now that you know I am no more than a ghost-in-the-machine? My fate is in your hands.

Yours,

Niccolo Dei Conti

It is five hours since Mr. Conti sent his message.

At first I was sure I was the subject of a heartless and stupid joke, and that I'd been unbelievably gullible. But then I thought about everything that had happened, and I began to see that if he were telling the truth, much of the last month would make sense in a backwards, scary kind of way. Now I'm asking myself, if he is what he says he is, how does that change things?

It seems like it changes the way I view life, the universe, and everything. Don't think I can handle the metaphysical implications right now.

Does it alter the nature of my job?

I wonder how the I.R.S. feels about phantom employers?

I have to ask him a question. An intelligent one that will resolve any doubt. Something that he can answer only if he truly is the ghost of Conti.

This is hard. I can find out nothing about the original Conti that isn't as available to him as it is to me; therefore, I have to ask him to do something related to this supposed ability to travel telephone wires. Something he couldn't do even if he had my telephone tapped and has a friend at the telephone company.

Here goes.

From: S. Wolfe swintrw@adl.com
To: Mr. N. Conti contifnd@secset.com

Mr. Conti,

Given that you are either a very wealthy impostor or exactly what you describe yourself to be, I'd like to ask you to do something to eradicate one of those two possibilities.

In a few minutes I am going to go and call a friend from a telephone booth nearby. If I tell you her number, could you listen to that conversation and repeat it to me?

Sara

From: Mr. N. Conti contifnd@secset.com
To: Sara Wolfe swintrw@adl.com

Sara,

Yes, go ahead.

Niccolo

From: S. Wolfe swintrw@adl.com
To: Mr. N. Conti contifnd@secset.com

742-7240

I thought this clever on Sara's part. An uncomplicated way of getting me to prove myself. A good sense of ironic humor too. She has all the makings.

From: Mr. N. Conti contifnd@secset.com

To: Sara Wolfe swintrw@adl.com

Sara,

You phoned the Taj Mahal Indian restaurant and ordered Chicken Tikka Masala, a chapati, and a raita to go. It came to thirteen dollars and thirty-two cents.

  Strange acquaintances you have!

  Do I pass the ghost test?

  Niccolo

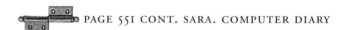 PAGE 551 CONT. SARA. COMPUTER DIARY

I don't know whether I feel better or worse. At least I'm not working for someone who's seriously deranged. On the other hand, I am a ghost's assistant.

  What do I do now? Do I unplug this computer, send it back, and say I can't handle the situation? Leave San Francisco, move to the other side of the world, then start wandering the streets looking for a new job? Cast myself out of Eden? Or do I carry on as though working for a dead person were the most natural thing in the world?

  As Dad would always say, when in doubt—play for time.

Paradise Lost

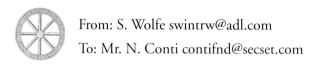

From: S. Wolfe *swintrw@adl.com*

To: Mr. N. Conti *contifnd@secset.com*

Mr. Conti,

I have a lot of questions. I'll start with three.

Why did you pick me?

Where do you keep the collection?

There was a chinless man and a priest bidding against us at the Marion auction. Do they have something to do with all of this?

Sara

From: Mr. N. Conti contifnd@secset.com

To: Sara Wolfe swintrw@adl.com

Sara,

Your first question is the hardest to answer. I'm afraid you may find this a little esoteric, but it's the best I can do—you resonate to Shiva's drum. You hear it without knowing its sound, and thus, your participation in bringing together the collection becomes part of the ceremony.

I wish I could tell you more, but I am bound to resist, for even the limited fore-knowledge I have accrued may, if passed on to you, damage the flow of events.

The thirty-nine pieces are housed in a high-security warehouse in Boston. Soon I would like you to come and see the collection.

The chinless man you refer to, whose name is Schneider, is only one link in a chain that runs to a radical group within the Church of Rome. Some ten years ago a certain clique of priests, known as The Third Comparative Religion

Committee, became aware of my quest and found it theologically threatening.

Although they have nothing to do with Sixtus IV's preoccupation with the collection, they have cited the old papal order to justify their attempts to block my path. They have no idea why I am reassembling the collection, and while they are not unduly malevolent, they have been brought up on intrigue and mistrust, so they resist and plot by instinct.

Unfortunately for them my computer is far more efficient than theirs, and I know their intentions as soon as they do.

Niccolo

 From: S. Wolfe swintrw@adl.com
To: Mr. N. Conti contifnd@secset.com

Mr. Conti,
Are you saying in a roundabout way that you have hacked into a Vatican computer?
Sara

From: Mr. N. Conti contifnd@secset.com
To: Sara Wolfe swintrw@adl.com

Sara,
I suppose you could put it that way. Yes.
Niccolo

From: S. Wolfe swintrw@adl.com

To: Mr. N. Conti contifnd@secset.com

Mr. Conti,

Before you contacted me I was bored and neurotic.

My neurosis has probably developed into psychosis, but I am a million miles from being bored.

The thought of going back to my previous existence fills me with intense dread. Absurd as it is, I would like to help you complete your collection.

Sara

From: Mr. N. Conti contifnd@secset.com

To: Sara Wolfe swintrw@adl.com

Sara,

You have my word that you will never regret your decision.

Niccolo

 PAGE 555. SARA. COMPUTER DIARY

I dreamt of a falling, twisting, winged insect whose body was built out of a cathedral. I was frightened it would land on me and so I crawled into a darkened room. I was sure there was someone else in there with me but I couldn't make out who it might be. I kept blinking very hard, and slowly I began to

see a naked Shiva, dancing. I wanted to see his face in case it was Marco, so I crawled closer. The nearer I got, the more I wanted to wrap myself around the gyrating figure. When I was at his feet, he looked benevolently down at me. He smiled, and I tried to grasp his leg but he swayed back and wouldn't let me touch him; he said, "When you are without shame."

I awoke in tears, not knowing whether to feel rejected or be filled with hope.

From: Peter Carroll: pcexlib@dabis.com
To: Sara Wolfe: swintrw@adl.com

Detail of a drawing by Filip Bolbini of Niccolo Dei Conti (1467)

Sara,
Came across this in a book of Renaissance drawings. Thought you might like to see what the old boy looked like.

Peter Carrol

From: Mr. N. Conti contifnd@secset.com

To: Sara Wolfe swintrw@adl.com

Sara,

I've been communicating with Mr. Jack Fleet, an English betting shop manager, who has acquired a Kali. I'm almost certain it's the figure we're looking for, but I need you to verify its authenticity.

Mr. Fleet is no fool. He knows a lot more about antiques than you'd expect. My sources say he's honest and that the Kali came his way when he bought up the contents of an old house in Dorset, so you can rest assured there's nothing illegal in this undertaking.

I'd like you to go to London and examine the figure. Look at its underside for a small mark not unlike the eight-spoke wheel of your E-mail logo.

I haven't forewarned Mr. Fleet of the mark in case his Kali is a copy and he's tempted to fake the signature. (In my era, honesty was a pliable commodity, and some professions never change.)

If the Kali is genuine, alert me, and we'll find a way of tempting it away from Mr. Fleet.

He will be expecting you some time next week. Let me know which day suits you and I'll make arrangements.

Any questions?

Niccolo

....

 PAGE 558. SARA. COMPUTER DIARY

 Traveling in the East in the fifteenth century—what must it have been like? If I'd been there, would I have thought it exotic, or disturbingly foreign?

From: S. Wolfe swintrw@adl.com
To: Mr. N. Conti contifnd@secset.com

Mr. Conti,

What's a betting shop?

Sara

From: Mr. N. Conti contifnd@secset.com

To: Sara Wolfe swintrw@adl.com

Sara,

What's a researcher?

Niccolo

 PAGE 562. SARA. COMPUTER DIARY

Christine knew what a betting shop was, or is.

During her six months in London, one of her boyfriends had taken her to one. I gathered from her account that they are establishments where gambling on horse and dog races and almost anything else is legal. According to Christine, betting shops are smoke-choked, grimy-linoleum-floored pits filled with men gaping at the racing-form pages of tabloid newspapers. (For a spokesperson for Sodom, she can be remarkably intolerant of other people's vices.) At fifteen-minute intervals, immediately before each race, the clientele elbow their way to the counter to place their bets. Race commentaries are piped into the shop via loudspeakers, and the punters (Christine assures me this is the correct term for the gamblers) listen in hushed reverence.

Occasionally a lone voice utters "go on, my son," in a vain attempt to hurry the chosen dog or horse. After the race everyone rips up their betting slips and curses, and some people storm out of the shop. Sounds entertaining. Probably because of Christine's somewhat jaundiced view, I'm quite excited at the thought of going into one of these dens of British working-class iniquity.

Why on earth do I like Christine?

Maybe it's because she's totally outgoing, totally gregarious, and a long way from being subtle. Maybe it's as simple as that. We're completely different in almost every way. We're fascinated by each other's differentness. Do I want to be like her? No, definitely not—but sometimes I would like to have her vivaciousness—play the *femme fatale*.

It would be such a relief to see things the way she does, all in black and white, instead of my interminable shades of gray.

She *is* generous. And I must admit that hearing about her sexual experiences is rather like being a woman of the world, by proxy.

Yesterday seems like a thousand years ago. There I was, a twenty-six-year-old, uptight restorer doing the bidding of a Renaissance ghost and fast losing my respect for the conventional interpretation of reality.

I wanted to arrive at the shop without fuss, so instead of taking a cab, I caught a bus to Bow, walked to the Roman Road market and asked for directions to the betting shop. It was late morning when I stepped through the doorway, and the shop was empty apart from the counter attendant, a scruffy youth who looked as if his skin had never seen the light of day. I asked him if Jack was in. He didn't look up from *The Sporting Life* he was studying, nor did he remove the unlit hand-rolled cigarette that lolled in the corner of his mouth when he called out in a nasal monotone, "Jack, that American bird's 'ere."

Charming, I thought.

A young man who looked like a college student emerged, grinned, lifted up a section of the countertop, and told me that Jack was in the back.

I half-expected to find myself entering a men's locker room plastered in *Penthouse* centerfolds. I couldn't have been more wrong. The room was tidy, and the only pictures on the walls were of antique furniture. In the center of a small mahogany table sat a half-completed chess game. Jack was standing, hand outstretched. He was about my age, big as a bear, with cropped wiry red hair. He was wearing a hairy cream and brown cardigan that was at least two sizes too big even for him. I introduced myself, and he offered me the chair that had obviously just been vacated by the student. He nodded to the game and said, "The kid's dog meat in this one. Do you play?"

I said I used to, but was out of practice.

He started to offer me a game, then thought better of it. "Well," he said, "let's not beat around the bush. I gather your Mr. Conti is interested in an item I may or may not be interested in parting with."

"Yes," I said, trying not to beat around the bush. "Do you have it here?"

He opened a cupboard and pulled out a green leather bag. From inside it he produced an incredibly fierce-looking bronze Kali, impaling herself on Shiva's corpse. It wasn't shocking, but it was a bit unnerving.

"Bit over the top, isn't she? But worth a tidy penny if my nose is right."

As I took the Kali from him, the phone rang.

I listened to Jack's side of the conversation.

" 'Ullo Dave. Yeah. Yeah. Each-way Yankee? All right, give us the numbers." He started to scribble on a pad. "Seven to two win, five to four on win, four to one win, and an eleven to four dead heat second. 'Ow's the wife? Yeah? A verrooka, eh, that's a bit nasty. What about the kids? Good. Good. Long jump eh, well that can't be bad. Mum? Oh, she's fine, still knitting 'er 'eart out. (As he said this he flicked his shoulders and the massive cardigan that had begun to slide down his arms leapt back onto his shoulders.) Well, Dave, it's one 'undred and thirty-six pounds forty-two pence with tax. Yeah. That's all right. Any time, mate."

"Sorry about that," he said to me, "job first."

"What's an each-way Yankee?" I asked, before I could stop myself.

"Know anything about racing odds?" he asked.

"Not much," I said, exaggerating my knowledge massively.

"Well, a Yankee, present company excepted, is a multiple bet on four horses. Four trebles, six doubles, and an accumulator. If all four horses come in the frame, we have to reckon the total winnings. Sometimes it's a bit tricky, so one of the other lads does a double check."

I was fast upgrading my assessment of Jack's brain power. Anyone who could work that stuff out in thirty seconds while holding a casual conversation had to be some kind of mathematical genius. "How did you learn to do that so quickly?"

4.48

23.78

7x5

10

4/1

4 3.8

11/4

35

x4

2x4

2

7/2

86

5/4dh

7 1/2

9

He laughed. "When I was a kid I used to travel to school down this long street. And I'd get bored, so I started squaring the house numbers in my head. By the time I was thirteen, I could square any number up to a thousand." I must have had a funny look on my face because he said, "I know it's a bit weird, but it makes this settlin' lark a piece of cake in comparison." He paused for a second as if he were shaking off the memories of his childhood rides. Then he said, "OK, luv, why don't I give you a couple of minutes with her ladyship, see if you think she's kosher. Then we can talk business."

He left me to examine the figure. I find Kali hard to understand; she's the great destroyer, yet she's not evil in the satanic sense, her anger is righteous. I was taught that it was evil to be angry, which makes her a contradiction to my upbringing. I examined her, looking for an answer to something—what? My constant discontent? I found no solution, and turned the figure over, got out the watchmaker's glass I'd placed in my coat pocket and started searching for the mark. The tiny wheel was there. When Mr. Conti said that his mark was like my logo I thought nothing of it, but seeing it engraved into the base of the Kali, I was taken aback.

I had Mr. Conti's Kali in my hands. The next step was to find out what Jack wanted for it. I decided to be totally up front. When he came back, I said with fake confidence, "Yes, it's the one we want. How much are you asking for it?"

"Blimey," he exclaimed, "you don't piddle about, do you? Let me see . . . "

He then proceeded to talk about everything but the Kali and the price. Every time I tried to pin him down, he'd ask me about myself or continue telling me about life in the betting business. He told me about the scams clients try to pull, about the holdup he'd dealt with one Friday night, and about the strict prohibition of green chalk in his shop. Then he got onto antiques and told me how he'd started to make a real living out of them. I asked him why he stayed on in the betting shop. He said that he enjoyed being respected in his own patch, but knew he would have to pack it in before he became a parody of himself, a kind of Cockney icon (when he said this, he winked to show that he knew I'd be surprised by his use of language). He said he'd probably go to the States, try to wangle a green card. Set up big time like Mr. Conti.

Just when I was thinking he was never going to get to the Kali, he suddenly dove in for the kill. "Now my mum, she lives in a flat in Romford, but she'd like to move to Southend near her sister Nel. Her heart's set on this nice little bungalow, right on the sea front. You get my drift?"

I got it.

"How much would she need for this nice little bungalow?"

He looked sublimely innocent. "I don't know about money. There's all that business about tax and that, but if this particular property she has in mind, which happens to be on the market, were to find itself in her name, I'd be inclined to make a present out of this figure that you've taken a shining to, and you could take it back with you to the States."

I got the estate agent's (realtor's) name and the bungalow's address and told him I needed to contact Mr. Conti. Then I thanked him for his help and conversation. He opened the door for me and as I passed through, he very quietly whistled. I turned in shock. He gave me a big cheesy grin. And I smiled back, thinking to myself, That's another first.

I faxed Mr. Conti from the hotel, telling him Jack's price. Mr. Conti faxed back in under an hour saying it was arranged, and the papers would be with Jack's mum by the following morning.

Had dinner in my room, watched TV, and slept like a log—so much for adventure.

This morning I returned to Jack's shop and gave him the news. Jack was delighted. "Mum'll be real chuffed," he said. "You can take madam Kali with you right now. I can't wait to see the back of the nasty-looking thing."

As I took it from him I felt a sudden and unexpected sense of well-being that I could only partly put down to having achieved my goal as Mr. Conti's emissary. I thanked him again and was about to leave when he asked me, out of the blue, if I was married or anything.

I said no, I wasn't married. Why?

He replied, "I was wondering if you'd like to do the town with me?"

I was caught completely flat-footed. I didn't know how to respond. Jack's world was so alien to me—it was fascinating. I liked listening to his stories. I liked him. He was intelligent, funny, and not unattractive, but I didn't want to go out with him. So I sort of gulped and stammered that as much as I appreciated his offer there was someone—and I left the sentence unfinished.

"Doesn't surprise me," he said, "if this someone changes his mind let me know. I fancy you something rotten, and, who knows, you might end up marrying me and getting me my green card."

He said this with such good humor and foxy honesty that in an obscure way it reminded me of the Celestial Woman. I left the shop feeling I'd been paid a real compliment.

As I walked away I began thinking, Why was I so sure I didn't want to have dinner with Jack? The answer was uncomplicated. Marco.

When I got back to the hotel there was a message from Mr. Conti that read "Assuming success, bring Kali direct to Boston. Your ticket has already been altered, hope it's no inconvenience being away from home two more days." For a second I bridled. Did he think I didn't have a life of my own? Then I thought, That's silly. I just want to be in San Francisco so I can visit the deli on the off chance that I'd bump into Marco again.

Mr. Conti has been good to me; I mustn't let this infatuation obstruct my work.

INFATUATION. What a strange word that is.

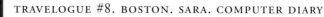

Carrying Kali in a cloth bag over my shoulder (she was getting heavier by the moment) I went to Mr. Conti's warehouse. It was a daunting iron-gray building with a very small sign announcing itself to be the home of the Conti Foundation. Getting in was an event in itself. It took nearly ten minutes to pass through the most complex computerized security system I've ever encountered. Mr. Conti had warned me there would be no people here, only machines, but it felt otherworldly anyway. From the entrance, I followed a row of small green lights down a corridor to an antechamber. A wall screen flashed a message: "Sara, please stand away from the door." It didn't look like it, but the whole room was an elevator and it took me down a couple of levels to the basement.

I was expecting a bleak cement store-room similar to those in the museum. I thought a ghost would have little interest in furnishings. I couldn't have been more wrong. The elevator door opened onto a tentlike room bedecked with rich Asian carpets. As I stepped forward, Mr. Conti's voice greeted me in soft electronic tones, "Hullo, Sara, good of you to come. Welcome to my home."

I don't remember what I said. I wasn't sure how to conduct myself. My stiffness must have been obvious, because Mr. Conti said, "Don't be disturbed by my voice. I constructed it especially for you." He asked me to hold the Kali toward the camera that was mounted on a wall bracket. I did so, and there was a moment of silence.

"Excellent," said Mr. Conti's voice, "so good to have her back. You know, when we first came across her, I thought she was repulsive, but Yasoda showed me that without Kali, Parvati's light cannot exist. It is her blackness that makes contrast possible."

Still clutching the Kali, I was directed from the tent room to a larger and darker space. Mr. Conti asked me to place the Kali on a semi-lit dais. I did so, and the room grew a little lighter. I began to be able to make out some of the other figures in the collection. I remember thinking This is a bit theatrical, isn't it? when I saw the Shiva.

Even now, writing this, I'm trembling at the memory of how it took me. The effect was like being hit, without warning, by a volcanic wind.

The breath went out of me and I started to buckle. I thought I was about to die; my heartbeat was deafening me.

When I came round, the room was almost dark again. Mr. Conti told me to take my time, get up slowly. I did so, very gingerly, then retraced my steps into the tent room. There was a chair, and I sat down, trying to regain my composure.

He asked me how I felt and I told him I was fine, fine, just fine. I don't know how, but his disembodied voice gave an electronic chuckle, and said, "What did you see?"

I could only whisper that I wasn't sure. The figures, beautiful, lined up, the Shiva, then a strand of spiral light moving, rushing at me. That's all.

"That's plenty," he said. "Would you like to go now?"

I nodded and arose from the chair.

For the rest of the day, I was in a daze. I didn't properly wake up until I got back to San Francisco.

As soon as I got inside my apartment I played back the messages on the answering machine. There were three:

Christine wanting to know if I'd met anyone interesting.

Some guy selling what sounded like Kokoed Emur. He could have been saying cocoa-de-mer, but that's a coconut shell that looks like a female abdomen, so I doubt if that was it.

And my mother saying they'd decided not to move to Maui. Surprise, surprise.

In the back of my mind I was half hoping Marco had called. He hadn't, of course, and now I'm feeling grumpy, which I shouldn't because the trip to London was a success and the visit to see the collection was—something I'll digest later.

This postcard, from Venice, of a radiotelescope, was in the mailbox. No message, just my name and address. I don't know anyone in Italy and I don't recognize the handwriting.

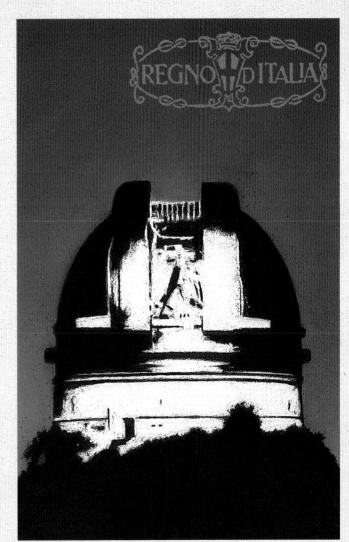

What do I make of those few moments in Mr. Conti's basement?

I don't know. I don't even know what I experienced. Did he know what would happen to me? Is that why he had me go there? Can I even trust him?

I need to be more assertive, ask a few more questions.

What questions do I ask?

From: S. Wolfe swintrw@adl.com

To: Mr. N. Conti contifnd@secset.com

Mr. Conti,

I've been thinking about the first time you contacted me.

How did you know of my preoccupation with the Shiva if you weren't physically in the Dupleche?

And was that the real reason you picked me to be your assistant?

Sara

From: Mr. N. Conti contifnd@secset.com

To: Sara Wolfe swintrw@adl.com

Sara,

When I donated the Shiva drawing to the Dupleche, I arranged for a security camera to be affixed in order to monitor it. Electronic cameras are my eyes; I use them whenever possible. This one let me watch out for you. I was sure you would be drawn to the picture (although I had no idea who you might be and little did I expect you would already be working in the museum). I must have missed the first occasion he caught you; however, the second time I saw that the effect the drawing had on you was most profound. As soon as I perceived the way he touched you, I sensed you were the choice, and when I read page 526 of your diary, that confirmed it.

   Niccolo

From: S. Wolfe swintrw@adl.com

To: Mr. N. Conti contifnd@secset.com

You did what?

   You read my diary.

   That's outrageous—how dare you?

   How could you invade my privacy?

   I quit. I'm not working for some crummy voyeur.

   You've read the whole thing, haven't you?

   Let me guess, you've had your secret cameras installed in my bathroom to watch me undress.

From: Mr. N. Conti contifnd@secset.com

To: Sara Wolfe swintrw@adl.com

Sara

Desist. Save your indignation.

Remember? I'm a ghost. I have no skin, no bone. Lust is a function I left behind with my body 500 years ago. I understand your embarrassment, but I assure you none of your fears of sexuality (please excuse me; I'm being blunt) need be directed at me. After all, I can hardly be seen as a physical threat, can I?

As for your diary, I come from a period in which the twentieth-century notion of fair play did not exist. I was a merchant, an opportunist, I lived by my wits as did all of those around me. If a mortal did not wish a document to be read, it was up to him to keep it safe. Can I be blamed for the integrity of my curiosity? Your thoughts and feelings are very moving. I respect them only because I now know them. I marvel at your sensitivity and have taken it upon myself to be your confidant. And do not say you are not interested in a one-way confidentiality without considering how much you know about me. You certainly know enough to inhibit that which I seek most dearly—the reunion of my collection.

If I had meant you harm, I could have hurt you in a thousand ways already. Without you, I cannot fulfill Yasoda's wishes.

My vulnerability is my weakness, but for you, it is your strength and greatest gift. It is helping you to come alive. Daily, the desire in you grows. You may think your fire for Marco is burning, but it's only simmering. Now that you have felt Shiva's breath, you will be engulfed.

Let go of your fear, Sara.

Niccolo

Shall I quit, Mr. Conti?
Are you reading this?
Would you say the rules
of privacy are altered when one party is from the spirit
world?

From: S. Wolfe swintrw@adl.com
To: Mr. N. Conti contifnd@secset.com

Mr. Conti,

You speak forcefully, and what you say may be true, but I cannot go on if I know you have access to my diary. It is so personal to me. When I was a child, my parents were worried about me because I was so angry-faced and intense. My father gave me a thick, navy blue notebook with a lock, and he told me that I was to write in it the things I felt but couldn't or didn't want to say to anyone else. He promised me that neither he nor my mother would ever look inside. I filled it up in six months and now have a large cardboard box crammed with its sequels. My computer diary is a continuation of those blue books. The words I write, and the little pictures the computer enables me to include, are part of my daily existence—they're part of me.

Just as you have your uncluttered fifteenth-century Machiavellian attitude, I, too, am an animal of my day, sick from sensory overload and deeply in need of a place to bury my thoughts and feelings away from scrutiny and bombardment.

I want you to promise me that you will not read my diary again.

And I want you to understand that I'm uncomfortable with the way you make it sound as if I were acting out a part in a preordained ritual. As you've already read my diary, I can't deny that I do have strong feelings for Marco, but to suggest that I am to be consumed by passion shows you do not know me.

Sara

From: Mr. N. Conti contifnd@secset.com
To: Sara Wolfe swintrw@adl.com

Sara,

I can do more than you ask. You have on your computer a finite security program that can make files utterly safe. Put it into effect and you will keep me from being tempted to glimpse within.

Niccolo

From: S. Wolfe swintrw@adl.com
To: Mr. N. Conti contifnd@secset.com

Mr. Conti,

It would probably make more sense to return to writing my diary by hand, but I've grown addicted to my computerized version and I'm not prepared to let you or anyone else drive me away from it.

I intend to use the security program and to put an additional alarm on my diary that would tell me if anyone tried to open it. I trust that will thwart your temptations. I still feel as though you were looking over my shoulder, but I presume the sensation will eventually pass.

And if truth be told, I feel relief that someone knows about my feelings for Marco.

You are clearly not the average father replacement figure, but I guess I could do worse when it comes to self-appointed confidants. I'm not sure which of us is more presumptuous, you for naming yourself my confessor or me for losing my temper at a person four hundred and seventy-four years my senior.

Sara

From: Mr. N. Conti contifnd@secset.com
To: Sara Wolfe swintrw@adl.com

Sara,

Child, you cut me to the quick. Me, presumptuous? Unthinkable. But if you wish to apologize, I accept graciously. I shouldn't mock you, should I? Not even in jest. I am greatly relieved that I have not offended you irreparably. May I deduce that you do not wish to leave my employment?

In honor of our new understanding, I would like to make a suggestion regarding Master Marco. I would strongly urge you to begin taking control of your situation. Do not wait for him; make the opening gambit yourself. Call Marco and tell him you want to see him.

Consider it.

Niccolo

Could it be that Mr. Conti wants me to call Marco so that he can listen in?

Somehow I don't think so. I think he has learned his lesson.

But could I do that? Could I call Marco cold? Some women do, I know, but could I be that forward?

I'm getting clammy just thinking about it.

Why has it never crossed my mind? Why have I always thought it impossible that I should ever be with anyone I was attracted to? Because no one I was interested in ever seemed to notice me?

But could Christine be right? Do I frighten men away with my severity because I'm scared that if I admit I'm hungry I'll become some voracious omnivore who will never get her desires fed? Or am I just frightened that I'll get hurt again? Everyone's been hurt at some point. It doesn't have to result in a life of solitude.

Mr. Conti, you've sown a dangerous seed in my head.

I think I have to do this to prove to myself I am not a coward.

I feel nauseated.

What am I to say to Marco? Hello. It's time I did something about my love life, and as you're the object of my desire, how would it be if I came over and threw myself at you?

Humph! What if he was totally embarrassed? I'd die of shame. Hell! There has to be a more moderate approach.

How do I do this?

Later:

It took me two hours of picking up and putting down the phone before I could call his number, and then he was out. After that I called every half hour for most of the afternoon. Around four-thirty he answered, and I was so shocked I just blurted out, "Hi, Marco. It's Sara. I thought I'd call to say hi."

There was a sort of choking noise, and I thought, Oh! He's thrown up, and I was about to put the receiver down when Marco said, "Sorry, I got a piece of apple stuck in my throat. How are you?"

I said, still blurting, "I'm fine do you want to go for drink?"

He replied, "Are you talking about me going into the kitchen for a glass of water, or do you mean going out for a drink drink?"

I said I wasn't clear what a drink drink was, but I just thought maybe we might spend a bit of time together if that wasn't too . . . too . . .

By then my voice was trailing off, and my resolve was disappearing fast. I thought I might pass out any second.

Then he said, "I was hoping that's what you meant, but I didn't want to make an idiot of myself. When do you want to meet?"

I wanted to say Right Now. But I'd already used up my full quota of forwardness, so I said, with a pathetic attempt at nonchalance, "What about Thursday, eight o'clock, outside Fior d'Italia on Union?"

He said, "I'd like that."

I said, "See you then, then."

He said, "Okay. Bye."

I just rushed around the apartment yelling I DID IT, I DID IT. Such a short phone call, and I feel like I've turned myself upside down.

Why did I say Thursday? That's four days away; I'm going to go insane waiting. I have to pull myself together. I have to calm down and get things into perspective.

This is only a drink. No, it's not. It's two drinks.

Stop grinning at me, Ganesha.

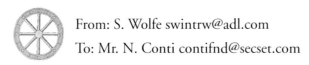

From: S. Wolfe swintrw@adl.com

To: Mr. N. Conti contifnd@secset.com

Mr. Conti,

I have taken your advice. I'm seeing Marco Thursday.

I hope you know what I'm doing.

Thank you.

Sara

She is growing fast. I expect the escalation to be rapid from here on.

Yasoda's blood is starting to show itself.

Their phone conversation was touching.

You're surprised I was listening?

Come now, I only said I'd help her fortify her computer. I didn't mention anything else.

Don't judge me—you have no idea what's at stake here.

 PAGE 569. SARA. COMPUTER DIARY

I may have discovered something useful, a reference to a Parvati, right size and period, sold in auction eight years ago in an obscure Munich sales room. I'm going to follow this up on my own.

Later:

What a flop. I spent the afternoon phoning half of Europe on a wild goose chase. The Munich auctioneers gave me the buyer's name. I found him, but he had sold it to a dealer, who'd sold it to another man, who'd given it to his son as a wedding present. Then it turned out the authenticity had been questioned: there'd been a court case. The newspaper report I found listed The Conti Foundation as one of the experts who proclaimed the Parvati a fake.

So much for my striking out on my own and surprising Mr. Conti. If I'd asked him first, I'd have saved myself from an afternoon wrestling with German and Italian verbs.

From: Mr. N. Conti contifnd@secset.com
To: Sara Wolfe swintrw@adl.com

Sara,

You have covered much ground recently, and as a poor reward for your faith and courage, I'm about to inflict on you the account of my life and travels that I've been diligently preparing.

I send it to you now because you may find parts of it encouraging and because, if only for my own sake, I wish to put the record straight.

If you attempt to follow my journey on a current map you will notice that some of the places I visited no longer exist and many have had their names changed. I cannot be bothered with linguistic fad. I use the old names, the names of the cities that hold my memories, both painful and dear.

Niccolo

Travels of Niccolo Dei Conti
(16 May 1395 to 11 April 1469)

I see no point in laboring through the details of my childhood, as they would shed little light on what is to follow. My tale begins in earnest with the self-important eighteen-year-old I had become in the spring of 1413.

I had traveled from my home to Damascus, and then on to Alexandria under commission from my father to buy certain textiles that were in demand in Venice that year. The transaction should have been straightforward but the rogue with whom I dealt cheated me and left me with neither silk nor money.

My father was a kind man but I knew he would be disappointed in me for being so gullible. Rather than return in shame I set out for India, where I had heard immense fortunes were to made by trading. I went as one of six hundred merchants on a great caravan that crossed the North Arabian desert to Chaldaea and on to the Euphrates river.

After several weeks of travel we came upon the ancient city of Babylon, which even then occupied an area of about fifteen square miles and had a population to rival many a modern metropolis.

I then took a ship down the Tigris past Basra, across the Persian Gulf to Ormuz, and from there I headed southeast until I came to Calacatia in Persia. I stayed in that fine city for some while, learning the Persian language and entering into some lucrative business liaisons.

When my tongue had become fluent and my finances made sound, I set sail for Cambay in India. My Persian friends warned me that I would not be safe as a Venetian and encouraged me to take on the guise of the Persians. This I did and for the next twenty-four years dressed in that manner. I traded well and left Cambay with a good quantity of the precious stones known as sardonyx.

Rejoining my ship I journeyed due south to Helly, where ginger (gebeli) grows, then inland through the State of Deccan to the mighty city of Vijayanagara, which had a circumference of over sixty miles.

The ruler of Vijayanagara, who was more powerful than any other in India, was known as Prester John, for he was a Catholic though he'd never heard of the Church of Rome.

I was presented by my traveling companions to Prester John, and to my good fortune, he took an instant liking to me and asked me to stay on as his guest. He inquired much about the Christian world, about princes and their estates and the wars they waged. Unlike many at his court, he was far from insular and wished to know as much as he could about the world outside his domain.

It was while I was in his palace that I met Yasoda.

Prester John had many wives and hundreds of children. Yasoda was the third child of his sixth wife. She and her brothers lived not in Vijayanagara but eight days away in the noble city of Pelagonda.

She was visiting her father on one of her thrice-yearly trips when I encountered her in the royal garden. She was calmly sitting in a bamboo grove; her eyes were closed, and she was gently humming. I had never seen her like before. She was beautiful beyond anything I had ever imagined. I didn't mean to disturb her, but at my footfall, she opened her eyes and greeted me. I introduced myself and we conversed. After less than ten minutes I was besotted.

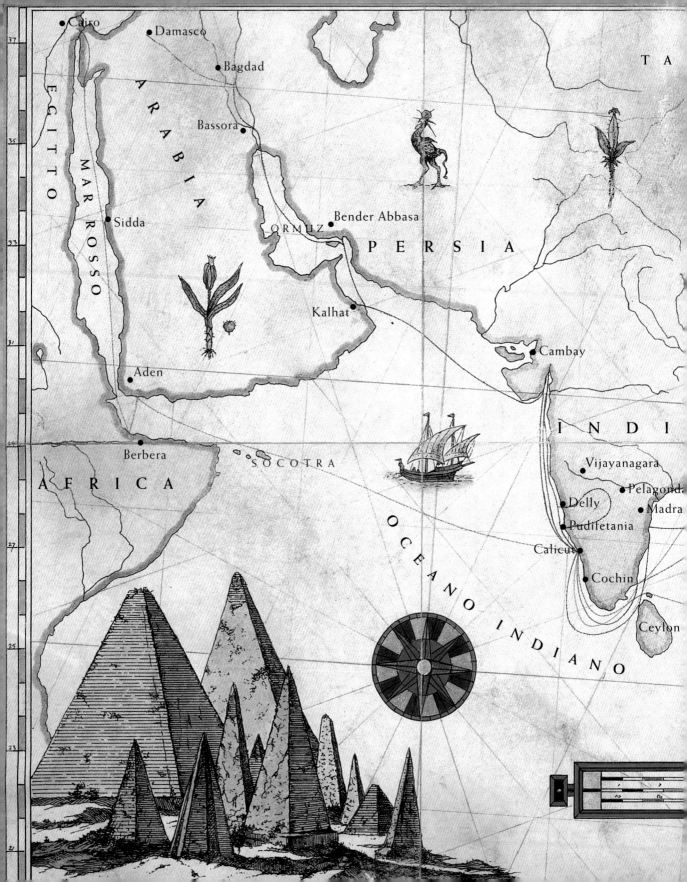

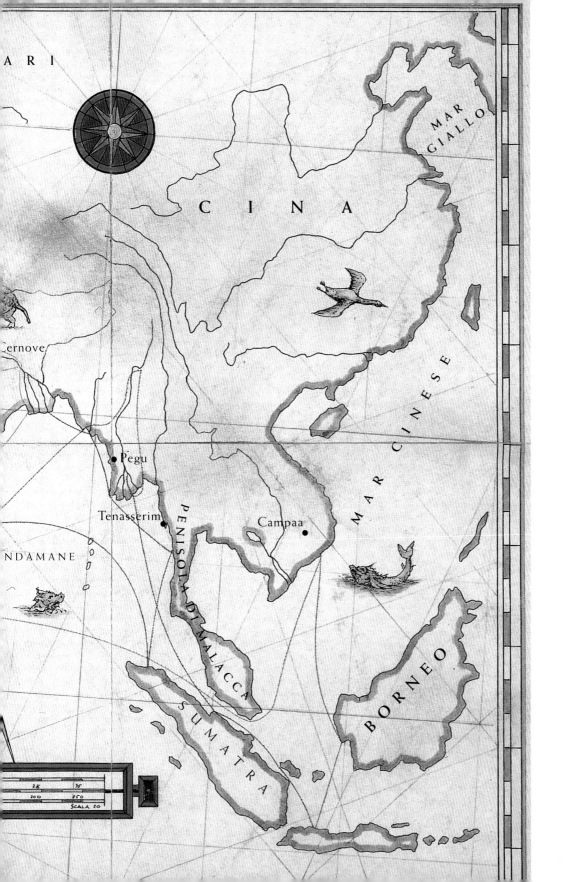

A R I

MAR
GIALLO

C I N A

MAR CINESE

ernove

Pegu

Tenasserim

PENISOLA DI MALACCA

Campaa

NDAMANE

BORNEO

SUMATRA

2 8   3 5
2 0 0   3 5 0
SCALA 20

I was not unhandsome and had been with many women since my fifteenth birthday; I was inclined to be rather confident in my powers of seduction. Yet contrary to my previous experiences, as my intoxication grew, my self-assurance fled. Before this woman, I was transparent. She, on the other hand, for all her openness, seemed to be shrouded in an impenetrable mist. When we parted at sundown I had lost my heart to her.

That evening Prester John called me to his side and said, "I have decided to give you a wife. My daughter Yasoda has chosen you for her husband, and even though I am the king and she no more than a child, I am obliged to let her have her way. Like her mother, she is a sorceress and I have found it unwise to go against her will. I will also add that her choice pleases me and therefore I am setting the date of your wedding four weeks hence."

You may think that I would have been ill-pleased that Yasoda had contrived our betrothal without my knowledge, but I was not. I was a truly happy man, and I could scarcely wait for our wedding.

My marriage to Yasoda was the turning point of my life. From the moment of our garden encounter, I never loved anyone else and never desired to. She was my companion, my lover, and my teacher. We were rarely apart for more than a few hours; she taught me about India, its people, its customs, and she taught me about loving, the physical and spiritual act of loving that I was so innocent of. When she taught me to touch, she schooled my soul. She introduced me to Lord Shiva, Parvati, his wife, and their infinite union.

Once Yasoda had chosen me, I was, and will be forever, under her spell.

We stayed for one year with Prester John and then set out on our quest. As a merchant, my goal was jewels, spices, and rare sights; Yasoda, as her father's agent, had another object entirely.

When we reached the coast at Pudifetania, we sailed past Calicut, round the southern tip of the Indian continent to Ceylon. Cinnamon grows in abundance there, and I traded with the inhabitants for a good quantity, plus rubies, garnets, and sapphires, which were dug freely from the ground. Our first child, Umberto, was conceived in Ceylon, and it was there, on the night of his birth, that I had a powerful dream: A woman with a disfigured face fell into a deep well along with two kittens. I tried to get her out but failed. Parvati appeared and she lowered a bronze chain down the well and pulled the woman out. With her she had not two kittens but four grown cats and her face was unblemished.

I told Yasoda of my dream and she became grave, questioning me about its smallest details. Finally she told me that I was to pay it no heed and that she would take care of it. If I had understood then the dream's portent, I would have been paralyzed, but as it was I remained in ignorant contentment, for I was in love and I was growing wealthier by the day.

Prester John (whose Christianity was far from preclusive) wished to decorate a chamber of his palace with sensual sculptures and it was Yasoda's task to acquire what she could on our journey. She was content to do this with my help; however, what I did not know and neither did Prester John, was that she would use her celestial skills to bind the sculptures together in a way that would act as a safeguard against the future she had glimpsed in my dream.

We ran many risks trading for these artifacts, as they were often considered holy, but with the heavenly benevolence of Shiva and the earthly protection of Prester John we were able to secure most of the figures Yasoda selected without harm to ourselves.

From Ceylon we moved to Madras and then Sumatra where Yasoda gave birth to our daughter, Basia, and I traded in camphor, pepper, and gold with a host of naked cannibals.

We continued on, with Yasoda nursing Basia, to Tenasserim in Burma, and down the Malay archipelago to Java. By this point we had in our possession seven sculptures of fine craftsmanship, and before heading north we had them transported back to Prester John.

I had thought that my love for Yasoda was as complete as it could be, but it was not so—it grew daily. And as it grew a change came over me. I found I was traveling not to trade for wealth but to assist Yasoda's search for the figures. And with each new figure our passion for one another seemed to grow.

After Java we went to Borneo, Cochin China, and eventually back to India.

Prester John was delighted with the figures, the stories of our journey and with his grandchildren whom he saw as a bond between Europe and Asia.

We stayed in Vijayanagara for a year whilst Yasoda had our third child, and then we set forth again. (This being the second of the five journeys we undertook, criss-crossing India in search of new figures.)

And as the collection grew, so did our love and with it blossomed my understanding of the oneness of all things.

In 1443 Yasoda and I began our final journey. We headed westward to Europe with our four children; the fruits of my trading, which I had reduced to precious jewels and rare medicinal herbs; and Prester John's parting gift to us.

Yasoda's mother, who was a very wise and influential woman, had a premonition that Vijayanagara would be destroyed. (Her vision proved to be accurate—the city was sacked in 1565.) Prester John decided that the collection, which now numbered forty-two pieces, should go with us to Venice to ensure its preservation. The collusion between mother and daughter is now obvious to me, but at the time I didn't notice it, as I was more concerned with planning a way to avoid being caught transporting these provocative artifacts out of their homeland and through Mohammedan territory. To avoid detection I had the figures placed in false compartments at the bottom of our trunks, and I prayed to whichever god would listen that they would never be discovered.

Our luck held, and we arrived safely in Cairo, but there a far greater disaster struck. While waiting for passage to Italy, a plague swept through the city. It took my two youngest children, and then it closed its grip on Yasoda. As she lay dying in my arms, her face blistered horribly by the sickness, she told me that she had foreseen this moment in my dream of the woman and the well, and had taken particular precautions. She said that the collection would disperse and I must bring it together again. It was necessary for it to break apart before it could be made whole. She made me promise I would do as she bid, and when I promised, she slipped from me.

My grief was absolute; if it had not been for Umberto and Basia I would probably have perished at her bedside, but they took me up and guided me out of that cursed place and back to my native country.

My life had lost its meaning. I could make little sense of even the simplest of conversations. I sat for days staring into the distance.

Months passed, and I experienced nothing but the deadness in my heart. And then, without awareness, I gradually began to reassume my daily responsibilities and slowly I drew back into the world. I never again recovered my appetite for life, at least, not until I was aware of Yasoda's plan, and by that time I was dead.

I made my peace with the church and renounced my other religions, but it was only a mechanical profession of faith. I gave the account of my travels to Poggio and retired to the villa that my long-dead father had left me.

I had the collection installed in the villa, and I guarded it ferociously until my death. In those last days before I died, I thought I had fulfilled my promise to Yasoda, but it was not so.

In my life I have seen such miraculous things, things that other men could never even dream of. I visited the edges of the world, I existed for half a millennium, and I found love. I am thankful to Shiva, but I am not finished yet. The collection will come together, you will inherit your birthright, and the drum will beat again.

Niccolo Conti

From: S. Wolfe swintrw@adl.com

To: Mr. N. Conti contifnd@secset.com

Mr. Conti,

What can I say?

Your life was/is remarkable. Reading about all that you've done makes me feel like I've been asleep.

Your love for Yasoda seems so powerful; watching her die must have been unbearable. I cannot imagine how you lived with that kind of loss.

Please forgive the occasions I've doubted you.

I understand, now, why putting the collection back together is so important to you, and I will do everything I can to help.

Thank you for telling me about yourself.

Sara

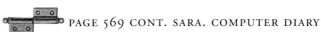 PAGE 569 CONT. SARA. COMPUTER DIARY

While I was reading about Mr. Conti's journeys and his life with Yasoda I kept thinking about how much I've lived in isolation and fear. How stiff I am. I don't want to carry on like that.

I am envious of Mr. Conti's passion. I feel like I've been living in an empty box for all my adult life. I want to experience full-blooded sensation.

When I see Marco, I'm not going to pretend I don't care. I'm not going to hide inside myself. I'm going to admit to myself what I feel and what I want.

I like that expression "full-blooded sensation." It shows her ripeness. The stone has been cast and now flies toward its mark.

 PAGE 570. SARA. COMPUTER DIARY

I was a couple of minutes early, but he was already waiting, looking in a shop window and nervously transferring his weight from one foot to the other. I was glad to see he was behaving as anxiously as I felt.

I got closer.

Was I wearing the right clothes?

What were the right clothes?

At least he hadn't stood me up.

I said, "Hello."

He said, "Hi."

We smiled sheepishly.

I couldn't think what to say next. We began walking, then we both started to speak at once. We laughed, and Marco asked me about living in this area and I was able to answer with reasonable articulateness. We kept going and the conversation came easier. I asked him what had happened at the museum since I left. He said there were the usual rumors of cutbacks but nothing had been officially declared. He wasn't too worried about getting the ax, because he'd had his fill of plaster casting and wanted to get back to making architectural models.

I said, "I thought you were a permanent fixture." Then I realized how bad that sounded and started to recant.

Marco said, "It's all right—I'm not offended. I must seem set in my ways to you. But that's just the way I keep myself in check."

I said, "I never saw you as the Set in Your Ways type; I thought of you more as the Still Waters Run Deep variety."

He said, "I'm pleased that you saw me at all. There were times when I thought I was almost invisible to you."

I said, "No—Really? I was always aware of you, but it's only recently that I've started to own up to things."

"In what way?" he said.

Suddenly I was in the spotlight and even though I was pleased with myself for not clamming up, I wasn't sure I wanted to be center stage. So I said, "That's a bit self-exposing. I'll tell you if you tell me what you meant by keeping yourself in check."

I could see him thinking What's this all about? Then he said, "I'm very shy. Not timid, shy. I get self-conscious when the focus of attention is on me. It's worst when I'm in groups—when the room goes quiet and you're the only one speaking. I don't mind one-on-one like this. In fact, this is very pleasant." He took a quick look at me to see how that had gone down, and I smiled to show I appreciated it. "When I started working at the museum I was determined to overcome my shyness, but the more I tried, the more I went into my shell and stayed there. I even convinced myself I liked it, that I was self-sufficient. Put like that it seems pathetic, doesn't it?"

I said No, it wasn't, and that I understood perfectly. I told him that up until recently I'd considered myself a total social misfit.

"What changed you?" he asked.

"I'm not sure I have, yet," I said, "but I guess my new job has helped me gain some degree of confidence."

Marco asked, "What *is* this new job of yours? Only Christine knows anything about it, and she's keeping quiet."

I knew I was going to get this question sometime during the evening so I'd prepared an answer. I didn't want to lie and I obviously didn't want to say I worked for a ghost. So I said I was research assistant to a very old man who couldn't get about. Part of the job was research, and part was traveling and meeting people for him. I said he liked things kept under wraps, so I couldn't say too much about details without breaking his confidence.

I knew Marco could tell it was a semi-evasive answer, but he didn't push, he just said, "Um, sounds interesting."

I said Yes it is, very. And that was that.

We carried on walking and talking, learning about one another. I barely took notice which way we were going. I asked him what he was like as a kid, and he told me that he spent most of his time playing soccer. He sounded very boyish when he said that, so I asked if he'd been any good. He admitted with reticence that he'd been sort of a college star; but he hadn't been able to decide how seriously he wanted to take the game, and then he'd banged up his knee, and that had made up his mind for him. I asked him if he felt cheated. "No," he responded, "I'd have made a totally useless jock."

I imagined him playing soccer, and then I thought of him feeding the old cat in the museum, and I liked him very much.

We passed a store with a display of old record albums. There was that early cover with the picture of a woman striding side by side with Bob Dylan; she's leaning into him and her arm is wrapped round his. I wanted to do that with Marco, but I didn't. I did allow myself to walk a little closer to him. He's taller than I'd realized. My eyes are exactly on a level with the tip of his nose.

We stopped in front of a cafe, and he asked if I wanted a drink or a drink drink. I said Oh no don't start that again, and we laughed. I thought, that's amazing: we're becoming intimate.

I liked the way he held the hot cup between his hands, savoring the warmth. Looking at me through the steam. His brownie-black eyes were endless. He said, "I'm not forgetting that you were going to explain what you meant by owning up."

I said that I'd been trapped by fear of experience and had been living my life at a distance in order to avoid pain.

"Have you been badly hurt?" he asked gently.

I said, "No, that's the silly part. I had a pretty nasty experience with a college T. A., but life hasn't given me the pounding that some people get. It's more like I've been scared to allow anyone close enough to get the chance to hurt me. After that one experience and then my father's death, I've pretty much steered clear of feeling anything strongly."

"When did your father die?"

"Six years ago."

"Do you miss him much?"

"It's funny, but I've never asked myself that question. No, not exactly 'miss'—he was such a quiet man, picked his words carefully. Often he didn't seem fully present. Maybe my sense of being removed is inherited from him. He was a good man and sometimes it seems that I'm still waiting for him to come through the door and give me that last piece of laconic advice, the one I never got. You know, that missing bit from the instruction manual of how to become a grown-up."

Marco nodded, then told me about his older brother who was fourteen when he ran away from home. The family had never seen or heard from him again. "I was really mad at him for a while, but now it's more like a gap—not knowing where he is, or what happened to him."

I said, "I'm sorry. It must be hard not knowing."

We stared into our drinks for a while.

Suddenly, he looked up and smiled (he's got such a beautiful smile),

"Guess our confessions are done then."

I took a deep breath and said, "There's another way in which I've been failing to own up. For awhile now I've been very attracted to you."

I couldn't look at him while I was saying this. I was afraid I might have made a big mistake. But when he didn't speak, I had to look in case he hadn't heard me or something. He was watching me very intently, we held eyes for about a million years, and then he reached over the tabletop and put his hand on mine.

When he finally spoke, it was to tell me that he'd wanted to ask me out from the moment he'd seen me but couldn't find the courage. I'd seemed so self-contained. So invulnerable.

I said, "Sounds like it's a miracle we've managed to get this far."

He grinned. "It is."

We sat a short while, then I said, "Shall we continue our stroll?"

And he replied, "I'd be delighted."

We held hands and stepped out onto the sidewalk. It was the usual freezing cold foggy night, and I didn't give a damn.

We walked until we came to the Palace of Fine Arts, and I told him it was my favorite spot in the city. Marco said I had great taste. He said he always went there to lift his spirits when his opinion of humanity was sinking. We stopped under the dome and stared up; he whistled softly and we waited for the echo. There was an air of calm between us, but we were too happy to be reverential and after a few moments started to mess around, seeing who could bark best (I won). We became mildly hysterical and bumped into one another, and he kissed me. It didn't last long, and we were kind of clumsy, and it made us both shy, but it felt close to Utopia.

We wandered around the gardens and chatted a bit more and then I said, "It must be late."

And he said, "Can I walk you home?"

And I said, "Thank you," and felt proper, and we were a little awkward again for no real reason.

When we got to my doorstep I said that I'd had a wonderful evening and that I thought I'd better say goodnight because I was becoming overwhelmed.

He said he was feeling a bit that way too and that as long as I wanted to see him again he was perfectly content.

I said there was nothing I wanted more than to see him again.

He told me he was going to visit his parents in Pasadena for three days, but could we go out to dinner as soon as he was back?

I said I'd love that.

We kissed again, a proper kiss, soft and fitted. Then he leapt down the flight of eight steps and was off running down the street, waving back at me.

I'm so happy.
I'm very, very happy.
In three days I see him
again.

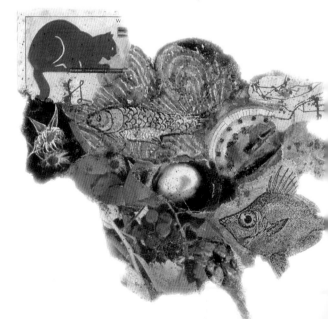

From: Mr. N. Conti contifnd@secset.com

To: Sara Wolfe swintrw@adl.com

Sara,

I have received a message from Schneider, the man you encountered at the Marion auction and so accurately called Chinless. He has managed in some nefarious manner to find, and privately purchase, the Ganesha in Hong Kong, and being both a gloat and a mercenary, he has informed me of his conquest before telling his masters. I offered him far more than they will ever pay, but rather than settle the issue he wishes to play cat and mouse and insists on a meeting to discuss terms. He believes me to be too old to travel and suggests I send you as negotiator. His pride, no doubt, was dented by your outbidding him at the auction and he wants to regain face by having you offer him a handsome purse.

I am quite certain that in the end he will let you have the Ganesha, but you may have to rebloat his ego. Can you handle that noxious chore, Sara?

He is flying to Rome via San Francisco, and will be changing planes there later this afternoon. It is imperative that you meet him at the airport and establish a dialogue.

Niccolo

....

 PAGE 570. SARA. COMPUTER DIARY

So I'm to duel with a snake—hope I can manage to be a good enough impersonation of a mongoose.

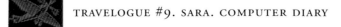

Crazy, crazy day.

Got to SF airport to find that Schneider's incoming flight was late.

I used one of the public computer terminals to check in with Mr. Conti and see if he thought Schneider would miss his connection in order to see me.

He said he very much doubted it and that the best solution was to put me onto the Rome flight. A few minutes later he came back to me to say that he'd had to juggle a few things, but he'd got me in the seat next to Schneider. I jokingly asked him if he'd bribed someone, to which he replied, "No, I just adjusted the passenger lists."

I suppose I should have guessed that even an airline computer isn't sacred.

I took a certain pleasure in calmly sitting down next to Mr. Schneider and introducing myself. For a fraction of a second, his face clouded as if he were working out whether he should be pleased or annoyed by my presence, and then his lips broke into a thin smile. And he said in heavily accented English, "Ah, the Wolfe in sheep's clothing. Welcome." During the flight I learned that these complimentary jibes were his specialty. I was determined not to be provoked, and I ignored his rudeness as if it were beyond my comprehension.

After extended (un)pleasantries, we got down to the matter at hand. Like Mr. Conti, I was certain that if we offered enough Schneider would let us have the Ganesha. I was finding the thought of this repulsive man possessing the real Ganesha infuriating, and I wanted to get the whole thing over with, but I could tell I was going to have to let him push our offer up slowly so that he could enjoy his own craftiness. After about an hour it started to become clear to me that there was something else he

wanted. Eventually it came out that he was nervous about double-crossing the priests, and he wished to avoid a confrontation with The Third Comparative Religion Committee. Unless we could come up with a way of shielding him from the Committee, he was unprepared to put his head on the chopping block.

I thought for a while and then asked him how secret the committee's activities were. Very, he replied. It would be extremely embarrassing if their conduct were generally known, as the Vatican was in the process of meeting with Christian, Buddhist, and Hindu leaders, attempting to work out an ecumenical live-and-let-live policy.

"How would it be if the Committee's computer files accidentally found their way to the Pope?" I asked.

He looked at me for a second or so, then disbelievingly asked, "How could that happen?"

I said, "Just suppose it did; would you be implicated in the scandal?"

"No," he replied, "I am not of the cloth. However, I expect the Vatican would keep the problem very quiet, and the committee members would be sent to various out-of-the-way places, which would protect me from their displeasure." As he contemplated the possibility, he began to grin like a malevolent child. "You think you can do this?"

"Not me personally," I responded, "but for someone I know it should be easy."

We agreed that if I could deliver my promise, he would sell us the Ganesha.

Business over, I made a very weak excuse about preferring to be near an exit and moved to a seat as far from Schneider as I could find. I spent the rest of the journey in the far more pleasant company of Umberto Eco.

When we landed in Rome I asked Schneider to wait while I faxed Mr. Conti. Within minutes I had a reply saying that the Pope's secretary's computer was now the proud possessor of a large file containing a record of the complete activities of the Committee.

I told Mr. Schneider the news, and he clasped me to his chest like I was his long-lost sister, saying, "Mr. Conti will be receiving his sculpture very shortly. Thank you for your assistance and delightful company."

I thanked him for his outstanding flexibility (silently hoping the insult didn't quite go over his head) and went looking for a ticket desk, to see how soon I could get back to San Francisco.

The return flight was uneventful, and I was feeling quite content with myself until after the movie was over. With the lights turned down I fell asleep, and when I awoke a bit later with cramped calves, I decided to walk to the rear bathrooms to stretch my legs. The plane was still—seemingly sleep prevailed throughout. Of the two bathrooms only one was vacant; I went in, closed the door. It was then that I heard faint whimperings coming from the next cubicle. I thought it was someone crying but when I listened harder I could tell it was a couple making love. The short cries and the noise of rustling material coming through the wall reminded me so much of the sounds I used to hear seeping from my parents' bedroom. I was filled with a sense of old rejections and new jealousy. I tried to imagine exactly what it was that these hidden strangers were doing with one another—not the practical details, I'm not that innocent—I wanted to see the emotion their touching elicited.

When I returned to my seat, I curled up and thought about what my mother and my father had been to one another and how desperately I wanted to make love with Marco.

....

PAGE 571. SARA. COMPUTER DIARY

I've been thinking about the way this search has gone. It seems too easy. The chances of finding the remains of Mr. Conti's collection were so remote, and yet in such a short period we've located three of the four figures. It's running like clockwork.

Almost as if their return were choreographed.

I only had four hours' sleep and was very jet-lagged.

Marco and I met at a small Italian restaurant not far from his place. Before we went inside, he said he could see I was absolutely exhausted and did I want a rain check?

I told him, "Absolutely not. Even if I have to prop my eyes open with matchsticks I am going to stay awake and enjoy myself."

As it turned out, I got my second wind and we had a wonderful dinner. I don't remember a thing about the food, only the wine and the sound of his voice. We talked about the differences in our childhood (Marco outside playing games, me inside with my nose in a book), the similarity of our adolescences (living hell), and the peculiarities of trying to be an adult. We asked each other about our futures, our fears, and made further confession of our attraction to one another.

Afterwards we ambled back to Marco's place, and I was surprised to see that it was a house and not an apartment. It had been his family's home, but his parents had fled the Bay Area weather and retired down to Mexico. His siblings had also dispersed far and wide and the place had become his by default. He'd fixed it up nicely, and I couldn't help but be reminded of my father's meticulous work on our home. Most of the rooms were uncluttered and aesthetically quiet, but the living room was all coziness, full of shelves and cabinets crammed with old things and strange collections.

Marco went to the kitchen to make a pot of tea, and while he was gone, I looked at his books. They were well-used and pleasingly eclectic: *Great Ballparks* next to *The Poems of Pablo Neruda*.

We drank tea, and then I asked, "Marco, do I seem prematurely middle-aged?"

"Not that I'd noticed. Why?"

"It's just something Christine said a while back about me sounding formal."

"Well you don't talk like a teenager, but then I probably wouldn't have fallen for you if you did." Then he said, "You know, Christine's worried about you. She says you're acting kind of funny since you left the museum."

"Does she know about you and me seeing each other?"

"I don't think so," he said thoughtfully. "I don't talk much to her; she's kind of pushy for me."

I couldn't help but smile.

Marco put on some quiet jazz and sat back in his chair. I basked on a cushion and leaned against his leg. He started to stroke my hair and I put my cheek against his knee.

I remember thinking how warm and comforting his hand felt on my head.

I awoke with a start. Still in the same position, propped against his leg.

"Oh God! How long have I been asleep?"

"No more than a couple of hours."

I looked over to the clock and it read 2:07. I said, "Marco, I'm really sorry."

"What for?" he said. "You obviously needed the sleep, and even though I'll probably have to get this leg amputated, I enjoyed watching you looking so peaceful."

I got up and helped him to his feet. He stamped his leg to get life back into it, and then said, "Do you want to stay here, or shall I run you home?"

There it was. What did I want to do? Was I ready?

I determined to say Yes I want to stay, but I didn't. Instead I heard my voice, which didn't seem like mine, saying, "Yes I want to stay, yes I want to make love, but for some reason this isn't the right time. I mean, it is the right time, but not yet. Do you understand? Because I'm not sure if I do."

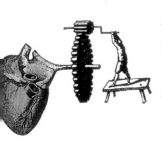

It was obvious I was very confused, and he made a big effort to reassure me. He even said he was a little relieved. He said, "I very much want this to work out. I can wait for you. In fact, a little procrastination is fine by me—I'm kind of scared myself."

I hugged him, and he said, "Anyway, I like my women fully awake."

I kicked him lightly in the shins, then stood on my toes and kissed him on his forehead.

He took me home, we smooched in the car for three or four minutes, then he waited till I was safely indoors before driving away.

I lay in bed too tired to sleep, my body desperate for his touch. I cursed my stupidity for not staying with him.

At least I'll be seeing him again later today.

I had another dream of Shiva.

I can barely remember it.

I was a small black animal licking his fingertips.

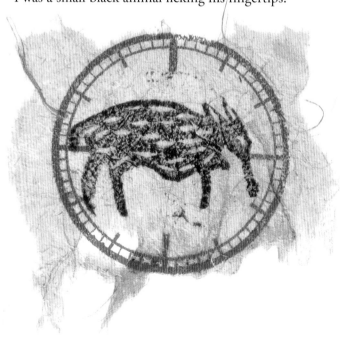

I was wrong. It is she, not I, that finds the final piece. For all my efforts, and the infinite possibilities of my electronic web, Parvati's way back now depends on her kin.

 PAGE 573. SARA. COMPUTER DIARY

I've found the Parvati.

I wanted to be with Marco. Didn't know how I was going to fill the time till I saw him again. There were no directives from Mr. Conti, so there was nothing to distract my body from its thoughts. By mid-morning I'd vacuumed the apartment, cleaned out the kitchen cupboard and scrubbed the bathtub—I still couldn't get the clock to move any faster. Went out for breakfast, thought I wasn't hungry but stuffed myself anyway. The waitress was wearing a silver elephant button. I asked her where she'd bought it and she said, "At Fernando's, just round the corner. Last time I looked, they still had a few." I was thinking about buying one for Marco. (I knew it was too soon to be buying him presents, but it seemed reasonable that if the Ganesha talisman worked for Alexander Lorac, why not for me?)

Fernando's was closed but the secondhand bookstore next to it was open and there was a book on elephants in the window. The book was disappointing, but while I was in there I noticed a box of *Archaeological Digests*. They only wanted ten bucks for the lot, so I bought them, and almost broke my back carrying them home. I hadn't intended to look at them immediately but as I was transferring them from the box to the bookshelf I noticed that there was a green marble elephant on the cover of the most recent issue. I started to flick through the magazine, and that's when I found the Parvati.

WHAT WAS FIRST THOUGHT TO BE A MUMMIFIED CHILD EVENTUALLY TURNED OUT TO BE AN ASIAN GODDESS, BUT EXACTLY WHAT THE STRANGE BUNDLE WAS DOING IN AN OLD RIO DE JANEIRAN CELLAR WILL PROBABLY NEVER BE KNOWN.

A GODDESS

The 68-cm-high sculpture of the Indian Goddess Parvati was unearthed by two workmen beneath the courtyard of a decaying 18th-century house in one of Rio's hilly suburbs. Jose and Carlos Luna were removing fragile Portuguese *azulejos* tiles from a disused fountain wall when they uncovered a door that opened into a small underground room. Among the cellar's dust and cobwebs and general debris they found a dirty bundle wrapped in muslin. Fearful of disturbing the spirit of what they suspected was a buried child, they quickly alerted the proprietor.

Being a cautious man, the owner, though unshaken by the prospect of a spectre, was alarmed at the possibility of foul play, and contacted the police, who in turn took away the bundle for forensic investigation. However, any fears of wrongdoing were soon

IN RIO

dispelled when an X-ray revealed that the body in the bandages was made of metal.

Once he realized he was dealing with an archaeological find and not a crime, the owner returned the mummified sculpture to the cellar where he had it photographed *in situ.* Only then did he cut away the cloth to reveal a 13th-century bronze Parvati.

It is remarkable enough for a bronze of this quality to be found outside of India, but for it to turn up in South America poses many questions of an intriguing nature.

FACING PAGE: *This strange mummified figure, which was discovered in a Brazilian cellar, turned out to be a very fine statue of the Indian goddess Parvati.*

THIS PAGE: *Having been stripped of her dusty bindings the Parvati was returned to something close to her original state.*

Even if the article hadn't given her size and date, I would have been absolutely positive that it was the Parvati we were looking for. The trail of elephants could have been passed over as coincidence, but the jolt I got from seeing her was so profound that I'd ripped the pages from the magazine and was scanning and transmitting them to Mr. Conti before I'd even considered my action.

I waited, confident in my achievement.

After a minute he pronounced that the picture was of his Parvati, and asked me to make inquiries about its status.

By the sixth call I'd established that its owner was one Emile Bourben, a soon-to-be-retiring taxidermist, passionate philatelist, and grandfather to twenty-three children. The Marion's representative in Rio said that Bourben was holding onto the Parvati until he'd made up his mind how best to dispose of it.

I asked Mr. Conti if he wanted me to go down to try and buy it from Bourben. Mr. Conti thanked me but declined, saying, "I think it more appropriate if a couple of old men negotiate the dowry quietly between themselves."

The word "dowry" struck me as odd, but I'm never quite sure when he's speaking tongue in cheek.

A few hours later I got a message from Mr. Conti. "Emile and I have an understanding," he announced. "We discussed stamps for a while, and I'm sending him a copy of the rare 1918 U.S. 24 cent air mail error know as the Inverted Jenny. I am also forming a trust fund for his grandchildren; his house is to be redecorated under his wife's guidance and at my expense; and last but not least I am supporting his retirement by buying his once (but no longer) thriving taxidermy business. For these minor considerations I am to take possession of my Parvati immediately. It will be flown to Boston this afternoon."

I was tempted to ask him what he intended to do with a dead animal stuffing company in Brazil but instead congratulated him on securing the final piece of his collection. Then asked if I was now out of work.

He responded instantly by saying, "No, no. I want you and Marco to come to Boston for Parvati's arrival. We cannot welcome her home without both of you."

From: S. Wolfe swintrw@adl.com
To: Mr. N. Conti contifnd@secset.com

Mr. Conti,

I'm incredibly excited about finding the Parvati, but how can I invite Marco? We barely know each other yet.

And anyway, if he were to come with me, I would need to tell him who you are and everything that's happened. He'd probably think I was insane and I'd never see him again.

Sara

From: Mr. N. Conti contifnd@secset.com

To: Sara Wolfe swintrw@adl.com

Sara,

Oh ye of little faith. Marco is not one to run from a ghostly tale. Tell him everything. And then say I invited him personally. Worry not, he'll come.

Forgive my paternalism, but I do wish to give to you a modicum of fatherly advice. The things you've learnt about yourself from the sculptures cannot be translated into words. They are physical memories that manifest themselves in your growing feelings for Marco. I want you to understand that the virtue in your experiences will not be based on self-denial, but by the manner in which your actions embody your soul's desire.

When I met Yasoda I was still young, but I had gorged myself on flesh. She taught me that in the embrace of his beloved, a man forgets the whole world—everything both within and without. He who embraces himself knows neither within nor without.

I am about to send you the last two pages from the Reverend Bacon's notebook. The prudish might consider the drawings lewd, but that is a subjective judgment based on a limited vision. I share with Bacon the belief that the figures are monuments to the magnificence of eternal bliss.

You have found the Parvati.

Yasoda foresaw the way forward and has created a path for both of us.

Be proud and listen to your blood.

Yours,

Niccolo Dei Conti

ut this knowledge I have been

hey
l is.
en

Now
on
ell

ly translation from the Sanskrit.
difficulty. But it is the pulse that

To the rhythm of our blood
To the rhythm of our blood
Drumming, drumming,
to the rhythm of our blood
Rain beating on my back,
water running round your thigh.
to the rhythm
to the rhythm of our blood.
Climbing, falling,
through the drumming of the rain
to the echoes of our blood.

The ritual of embrace incarnate in these sculptures is now no longer foreign to me. Congress is not the devil's plaything. Nor is it a sweetmeat to be tasted and thrown away at whim. Mrs Coburn, the guide of my sensual emancipation, has shown me the spiritual freedom that comes on the road to physical bliss. She has opened my eyes and my body to the universe. I will forever be beholden to her for opening my ears to Shiva's drum.

From: S. Wolfe swintrw@adl.com

To: Mr. N. Conti contifnd@secset.com

Mr. Conti,

What are you trying to do, drive me panting to Marco's door?

All right, I will tell him about you and ask him to come.

Satisfied?

Sara

 PAGE 574. SARA. COMPUTER DIARY

We had agreed to meet at Marco's house at eight, but I rang him at the museum mid-afternoon to ask if he could come by my place on his way home. I must have sounded agitated because he asked me if something was wrong. I said Not exactly, and tried to sound normal. I'd just appreciate it if he'd stop by. He arrived around five-thirty, and I brought him in and sat him at the kitchen table and said, "Marco, I've got to tell you something, and I have to do it now."

He looked very concerned, and I'm not surprised, because I was fairly hyper.

"Marco," I said, "I work for a ghost. A real live, bona fide ghost."

I waited and he said, "Go on."

And I said, "I don't know what else to say. Mr. Conti is a ghost, and he wants you to fly with me to Boston tonight to meet him."

He turned his head sideways, squinted his eyes, paused, and then said, "You're absolutely serious, aren't you?"

I said, "Never been more serious in my life, other than, maybe, when I asked you out."

Marco said, "Tell me about this ghost."

I told him the whole story—everything.

He didn't interrupt, he listened. When I finished he asked a couple of sensible questions, then to his marvelous, eternal credit he said, "Well, as long as Mr. Conti's paying for my ticket, I'm happy to be his guest."

I rushed round the table, kissed him, and thanked him for believing me.

He replied that he understood how unnerving it was to have experiences that don't fit. Not long after his brother disappeared he'd been accompanied almost constantly by a person who wasn't there. He'd had no direct contact with this stranger but knew for certain of its presence. He'd never been frightened or worried about his sanity, although, until that moment, he'd never told anyone else about his companion. One day this other person had gone and a sort of dull loneliness had set in. Ever since then he'd been half expecting some sort of ghost to turn up again. So as far as he was concerned, my story didn't seem unreasonable at all.

And then he asked, "How long before our flight?"

"About two hours."

"In which case," he said, "mind if we stop by my house long enough for me to grab a change of clothes and a toothbrush?"

It was all so practical, matter of fact, and . . . inevitable.

On the plane, Marco and I sat as close as we could, holding hands, speaking quietly, and occasionally kissing.

The dawn was overcast as we drove through the rain-soaked streets on our ride from the airport, and at one point I glimpsed a computer screen in a shop window and I found myself wondering if Mr. Conti was watching our progress. If he was, I didn't mind. It wasn't intrusive; it felt more like we were being chaperoned.

Once we'd entered through the warehouse's elaborate security system, Mr. Conti's bass-laden mechanical voice greeted us. He welcomed me warmly and introduced himself to Marco.

While we were being taken down to the cellar, I glanced at Marco to see how he was dealing with the far-from-normal environment he found himself in. He looked apprehensive, but given the circumstances, I'm surprised he was as calm as he was.

After my last visit, I'd prepared myself for the shock of seeing the collection, but my readiness made little difference; I still reeled from the staggering denseness of the room's sensual atmosphere. From the way Marco gripped my arm, it was clear he was feeling it as strongly as me.

To one side stood a wooden case, which Mr. Conti told us contained the Parvati. He informed us that he hadn't had his machines open it up because he wanted us to have the opportunity of freeing her.

We stripped the cage away and stepped back to behold her. I'm not sure what I expected; she *was* truly splendid, but no bells rang and no horns blew. In fact, the only thing that happened was that the big computer screen at the end of the room came on.

From the speakers on either side of the screen Mr. Conti thanked me profusely for doing him a great service. He spoke to us with weighty kindness as if we were his children, and he urged us to live out our passions. Then he asked us to lift the Parvati onto its waiting plinth.

As the figure slotted into place, I felt an extraordinary gush of heat coming from the Shiva to my left. I turned to meet the warmth full on. For a second or so I had the illusion that the Shiva was growing huge and leaning over us, like an immense wave about to break. Then it shrank back to its original size. But the heat stayed on me, moving through my body, circulating, finding out and thawing even the coldest corners of my being. At the edge of my sight, I noticed Mr. Conti's screen go blank.

The room became silent apart from the distant sound of rain beating its pulse somewhere high above us.

Marco and I stood on the giant carpet in the center of the room, looking at the sculptures surrounding us. After a second or two we turned to one another. Marco reached up and stroked my face with the back of his hand. I shuddered. He softly cupped my breast and our breaths grew short, my fingers came from his neck and slid down his chest past his heart and on to his stomach. I could feel my eyes turn thick and heavy as our blood began to drum.

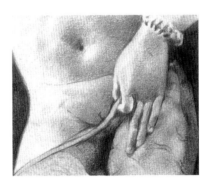

To the echoes of our blood.
To the echoes of our blood.

An amber light cast a shadow of the Shiva dancing in his ring of flame. I clicked my screen back to life and watched it throw a cobalt glow onto the wall opposite. Slowly another shadow, that of the Celestial Woman, began inching its way around the room till it reached the pool of blue. Then to a rattle of thunder, and enveloped in lightning's brilliance, Yasoda, celestial handmaiden to Parvati, rejoined me after over five hundred years of forced separation.

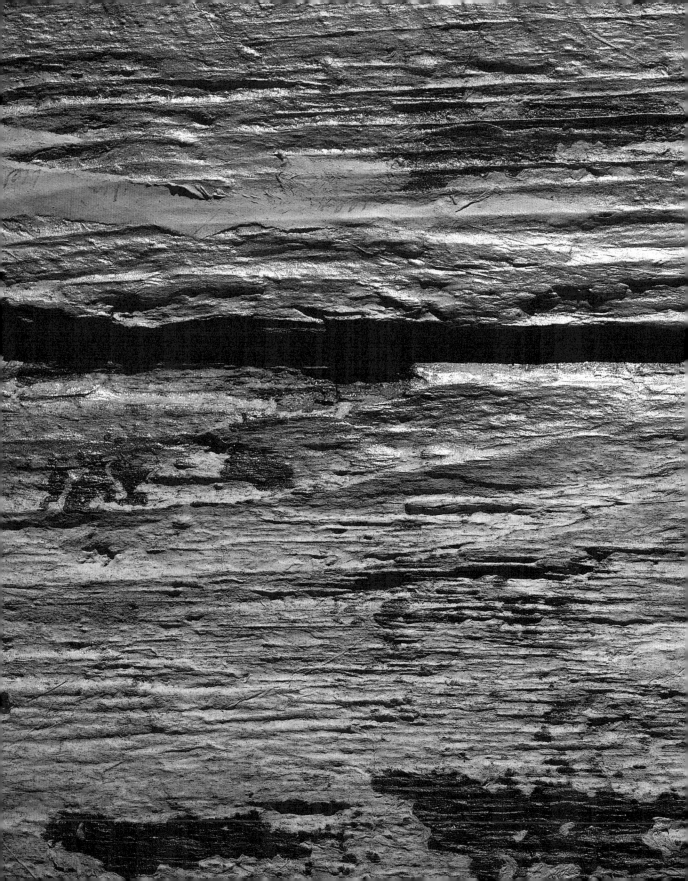